SLINGSHOT

Pete —
Thanks for your
interest. All
the best,

Ed

SLINGSHOT

Based on Actual Events

Edward Vick

Cover: Fire Fight Mekong Delta, R.G. Smith, 1969, U.S.
Navy Archives

Bedford Press
P.O. Box 504
Bedford, New York 10506

To order additional copies of this book, contact:
Xlibris Corporation
1-888-795-4274
www.Xlibris.com
Orders@Xlibris.com
16478-VICK

For Josh, Charlie, Jane
and, of course,
all the River Rats

PREFACE

River Patrol Boats, or PBRs, were the PT boats of Vietnam: get in close, interdict, disrupt and, if necessary, kill. The Navy's River Patrol Force was one of the most amazing units to serve in Vietnam. I still can't believe that I was ever a part of it.

This is a story about one mission in a River Patrol Force operation called Giant Slingshot in the Mekong Delta. It is based on real events. I first committed it to paper in 1970, shortly after I left the Navy. I was pretty angry at the time. I had volunteered for the Force and, like all of my comrades there, I did my best. But who was kidding whom?

By the late 1960's we weren't trying to win the war. We weren't trying to make South Vietnam free for democracy. The politicians were just trying to get America the hell out of there without 150 million voters noticing that we had spent a lot of human capital, and for nothing. We were going to abandon our Vietnamese allies and those Vietnamese civilians who believed in us. But we couldn't steal away in the night. We had to try to save some face. We couldn't make it look like a bunch of guys fleeing a bank job. So we took our time. We bought time. We bought it with the lives of the kids the politicians sent over there. What a waste.

Now, over thirty years later, I am publishing this story for several reasons. First, as a record for myself and for those with whom I served. This is not great literature. It's a war story. But half the profits from sales will go to organizations that benefit veterans of the River Patrol Force or their kin.

Second, I am publishing it for my family, as another sort of record. My great-great grandfather fought at Gettysburg, my grandfather served in the Army in World War I, and my dad was a hero in the battle for Okinawa. I wish I had some kind of feeling for what really happened in those places, where history was made the hard way.

And finally, I put this story in writing because every single young man with whom I served was a hero, and people should know that. In combat or out of it, I never saw the drugs, disloyalty or cowardice that too many people still like to associate with Vietnam's soldiers. I think most of that stuff was actually happening in Washington.

Did Vietnam make us is some ways insane, at least at the time? Of course. But anyone who wasn't there, as a soldier, a sailor, a pilot, or whatever, has no right to judge.

By way of a little color commentary, a few words about River Patrol Boats (PBRs) and Operation Giant Slingshot.

PBRs were thirty-two feet long, made of fiberglass and carried a crew of four (five including the Patrol Officer in charge). Each boat also carried a lot of weapons, from machine guns and grenade launchers to sawed-off shotguns and pistols. Fast, maneuverable and deadly, the PBR was first immortalized in Francis Ford Coppola's movie "Apocalypse Now." That surreal film was nothing like an actual PBR mission. This story is based on a mission that really did happen.

A PBR carried hardly any armor. No armor kept weight down. Instead, a boat relied on speed and firepower for both offense and defense. These boats of the River Patrol Force were introduced into Vietnam in 1965 as yet another means of interdicting illegal and hostile water traffic. Fully half of everything and everybody that travels and trades in the Mekong Delta of southern Vietnam still does so by water, along rivers and canals and, during the rainy season, even right across the millions of acres of rice paddies.

By 1968, the infamous Tet offensive notwithstanding, the heart of the southern Mekong Delta was thought to be pretty much under the control of the U.S. and South Vietnamese forces. So we all pushed further out, mostly to the west and northwest, away from Saigon and toward Cambodia, to expand the geography under "friendly" control. For the River Patrol Force, this expansion of operations meant that our fast but vulnerable little boats were being sent into narrow rivers and canals where the advantages of their speed was somewhat neutralized—for example, if ambushed, they could hardly turn around without stopping and backing up. And in the vernacular of the time, these new patrol areas were far from "pacified."

A number of these areas were declared, at one time or another, Free Fire Zones. In Free Fire Zones the Rules of Engagement which, for example, called for Americans not to fire unless fired upon, were eased a bit. Still, it almost seemed that we weren't supposed to win. We seldom had true initiative, and few combat units were ever really unleashed. And in PBR operations like Giant Slingshot, which is the setting for the mission I wrote about here, the Force took nearly fifty per cent casualties. Nearly half the boat crews ended up dead or wounded or missing-in-action. Astounding just to think about that one statistic alone.

But even more astounding to me was that, against this backdrop of blundering politicians, murderous firefights and bad statistics, the River Patrol Force to the end remained largely volunteers. As if that were not amazing enough, fully one-third of the Force's sailors signed on to extend their tour of duty when their one-year commitment was up. (I was not one of them.)

Finally I should note, with melancholy pride, that the River Divisions that took part in Operation Giant Slingshot were later awarded the Presidential Unit Citation, to this day the highest honor that an American military unit can receive for its actions in combat.

Bedford, New York
July, 2002

"There is often a very strange line between a medal and a court martial."

Unwritten tenet of the Navy's
Judge Advocate General (JAG) Corps

"The politicians can talk all they want about how Vietnam ain't a real war, but when a fifty-one caliber round takes off the fucking head of one of my crewmen, well, it's damn sure real enough for us."

Walter Hagren
Boatswain's Mate First Class
PBR Boat Captain
United States Navy

ONE

Yard Repair Base (Mobile)-14
Vam Co River
Republic of Vietnam
2330, 24 December 1968

"Merry Goddamn Christmas," the tired young sailor muttered as he looked up from his work.

The other two men of the boat's crew turned from the spindly plastic Christmas tree and watched their leader, a young Petty Officer, make his way down the ladder from the huge floating barge onto the pontoon dock to which their PBR was moored. With the light of a near-full moon washing over the blacked-out barge, they could clearly see that over his shoulder were slung a flak jacket and gun belt. They were getting under way.

"Saddle up, gentlemen," Petty Officer Shuster bellowed cheerfully. "Christmas is for pussies anyway. How 'bout we stow that Goddamn ugly excuse for a tree."

"Where we goin', Neil?" asked the youngest of the three crewmen.

"You know where, numb nuts. Up the river. Martin is up at Tra Cu with a crapped-out engine. So we're his relief."

Within minutes, the electrician's tape that had wrapped the tiny tree to the stanchion on the canopy top was stripped away. A short flagstaff took its place, and the American ensign fluttered in the steamy breeze that meandered down the wide river. Shuster stepped down into his Coxswain's Flat and lit off one big diesel and then the other. They idled dully as the crew began to move automatically through the routine that proceeded every combat patrol. Shuster flicked on the Raytheon 1900 radar, and its eerie green glow began to emerge. The radios came to life with purposeful, cloaked exchanges.

Automatic weapon rounds slid into their breeches. The forward gunner, sitting in his fifty caliber gun tub, jacked the handles on his powerful weapons, chambering rounds. Shuster himself strapped on his pistol and checked its cylinder. He then loaded two shells into a sawed-off shotgun that he always kept nearby.

With little talk and less wasted motion, the forward and aft lines were taken in and the smallest vessel that could legitimately be called a warship of the United States Navy was under way.

Thirty-two feet long and made mainly of fiberglass, the "Patrol Boat, River," or PBR, was propelled by two big General Motors diesels driving Jacuzzi waterjet pumps. For speed, it carried precious little armor, but the boat and the men on board were armed to the teeth. Speed and firepower were their offensive weapons, as well as their only means of defense.

Shuster commanded the boat and its crew of three. He went into battle wearing torn fatigue trousers, an old green T-shirt under his flak jacket, a ratty red bandana around his neck and a black beret that was the trademark of the Navy's River Patrol Force in Vietnam. He carried a long-barrel Colt non-issue .38 on his hip in a black holster. His dress reflected the fact that very few senior officers made their way to the places where Shuster and his crew spent their days, and nights.

His twelve-gauge shotgun fired tiny steel arrows called flachettes that could pin a gook to a tree. His steel helmet rested above his control panel. On the front of it, "Fuck you Charlie" was scribbled in marker. But on the back, in the same marker, "You and me, right God?"

Pulling away from the side of the hulking berthing and repair barge, Shuster maneuvered his PBR in behind two others also headed up river. He pushed his throttles forward gradually until they hit the stops. The boat rose up out of the water, on plane or "step" as the sailors called it, and headed northwest.

Ten minutes later, the Vam Co Dong River hove into sight off the starboard bow. The three patrol boats were still running single file, at full speed, with Shuster bringing up the rear. About twenty yards separated each boat. Shuster gripped the wheel a little tighter as he watched the two boats ahead of his, their dark green hulls black in the moonlight, roll to starboard and begin their sweeping right-hand turns into the Vam Co Dong. One right behind the other, the wake the boats made curved gracefully, white and silvery. With hardly a second thought, Shuster began to pull his helm to starboard. His boat leaned into the turn, kicking wake water high in the air off its port quarter. Shuster continued to turn the wheel, tightening the radius of his turn. The PBR sliced into the center of the mouth of the Vam Co Dong River, precisely in the wake of the two boats ahead, then flattened out as Shuster righted his wheel and all three boats sped up the narrow and very dangerous river.

Thirty yards wide at its widest point, the Vam Co Dong was a vicious little river. It bent and twisted unpredictably. Few straight-aways meant short sight lines. Surprise was around the next turn. There always seemed to be too much cover for the enemy and not enough cover for the good guys. Overgrown vegetation mixed with the defoliated product of Agent Orange. No part of this river could be trusted. It was crawling with Viet Cong guerillas and soldiers of the regular North Vietnamese Army or NVA.

The Vam Co Dong (Dong for "east") and the Vam Co Tay ("west") were the two tributaries feeding into the wide and now pacified Vam Co River which, in turn, flowed through the southern Mekong Delta and into the South China Sea. The Dong and the Tay flowed from two different angles, bracketing a piece of Cambodia called the Parrot's Beak, which protruded sharply eastward into the Mekong Delta of South Vietnam. Where the Vam Co Dong and the Vam Co Tay joined the Vam Co resembled a slingshot. Patrolling and attempting to control or "pacify" these two very hostile rivers had been dubbed Operation Giant Slingshot. Unlike all the main waterways in the Delta, the rivers further west and northwest, toward Cambodia, were not pacified. The Vam Co Dong was still, in every way, what the Rules of Engagement referred to as a Free Fire

Zone. And by Christmas 1968, the Vam Co Dong had already established itself as the deadliest Operating Area in the four-year history of the River Patrol Force.

Shuster's PBR 717, a new Mark II version of the original workhorse introduced in 1965, ran fast and clean up the river. It cut through rushing fetid air, which always smelled somehow ominous, under a too bright moon.

Twenty-two minutes later, and just into the "Christmas cease-fire" declared by President Nixon, Shuster saw the left bank of the river ahead erupt in a barrage of mixed fire.

"Holy shit," he bellowed. "Ambush! Left on bank! On the guns!"

First the sparking tails of B-40 rocket-propelled grenades flashed from left to right as they targeted the leading boat of the three. Two rockets swooshed over the top of that boat and detonated in the jungle off to starboard. One zoomed too far ahead of the patrol altogether. One just missed astern of the leader and nearly took off the bow of the second PBR.

One rocket was aimed too low, but it skimmed off the water and disappeared into the side of the lead boat. A split second later, its explosion lit up the PBR. The gunner amidships had just opened fire when the blast picked him up and blew him into the fast-moving muddy current, gone probably forever. The gunner in the stern of the lead boat also disappeared—somewhere—in the blast.

The boat veered to starboard, as though to flee the attack, but in a river only thirty yards wide, there was nowhere to go. The entire riverbank was now alive with fire as tracers flew out from seemingly everywhere. The second boat and Shuster's were now also under fire.

On board all the boats, every gun was returning fire.

The staccato hammering rose and rose in intensity. Tracers—red, green, white—arched and darted everywhere, almost beautiful in the moonlit dark. Occasional screams punctuated the non-stop firing. Smoke swirled around the PBRs and hung in the long tree line, amid the many hostile muzzle flashes.

Another rocket hit the lead boat, already crippled and slowing. The second boat, now only a few yards in front of Shuster as the sinking leader slowed the whole column, was being raked by machine gun fire. It was so close that Shuster could see the white bits of fiberglass under the green-painted hull fly into the air as bullets chewed it up. The Viet Cong gunner seemed to walk his rounds up the side of the PBR. A few pinged off the splinter shield around the Coxswain, then his head exploded sideways as a bullet caught it square in the left temple. He was slammed against the opposite side of his Coxswain's Flat, and the PBR slewed violently to starboard as he fell under the wheel. Quickly, the mid-ships gunner hopped down into the Flat and grabbed the wheel, steering the boat back on course.

The firefight lasted only a few minutes. Within thirty seconds the PBR crewmen, with superior weapons, better training and no alternatives, established that greatest of all Vietnam firefight states: "fire superiority." Though still exposed, with one boat sinking and still in the kill zone, they began to get the situation in hand. VC fire became erratic as the guerillas kept firing, but with their heads down.

Shuster's boat was the last one out of the kill zone. A final B-40 rocket streamed after his boat as it pulled clear of the zone and approached the safety of a bend in the river. As though magnetically attracted, the rocket seemed to seek out Shuster's boat, and Shuster. It entered the Coxswain's Flat from astern, just between two splinter shields, and detonated against the radios and radar screen, two feet to the right of where Shuster was standing, at his helm. He was virtually shredded, and he died instantly.

TWO

U. S. Navy River Patrol Force
Advanced Tactical Support Base
Tra Cu, Republic of Vietnam
25 December 1968

The worn fiberglass bow of the dark green PBR struck the mud canal bank, rode up onto the shaggy grass, then slid easily back into the water. The forward machine gunner moved around his mount on the bow and threw the aluminum anchor into the tangle of barbed wire that lay along the length of the canal, at the outer perimeter of the camp. The wire was in place to keep Viet Cong sappers from slithering up out of the canal at night and infiltrating the camp with their explosives. He pulled in the slack on the anchor line, took a couple of turns around a cleat and pulled is hand across his throat, motioning the Coxswain to cut the engines.

Lieutenant Junior Grade Jack Morelly hopped off the bow, over the wire, and walked quickly along the bank, toward the entrance to the camp. At the decaying wood and wire gate the old Vietnamese sentry, seated on a gray metal folding chair, grinned widely at him through dark and rotting teeth. He held a stick for a cane, but no weapon. His left eyelid had long ago been sewn shut, but his right eye watched Morelly carefully through its nearly opaque covering of gray glaucomic slime.

Kicking up powdery dust from the deep truck-tire ruts, Morelly walked across the campground toward the radio hut, designated the Naval Operations Center, or NOC, by Lieutenant Franklin, Morelly's Division Commander.

The low-clearance doorway had obviously not been constructed for a westerner. As he entered, Morelly could hear the Vietnamese officers babbling urgently off to his left in their section of the NOC. Nothing important was happening, he concluded, for if it were, they would not be talking. They would be wondering what the fuck to do next.

"Hello there, Post."

The radioman looked up from his dog-eared copy of *Dude* magazine as Morelly walked through the door. "Hey, morning sir. And a very merry freaking Christmas to you, sir. You bring the mail?"

"Yeah, merry Christmas to you too. Hagren's got the mail on the boat. He'll be up in a minute. I'm sure you didn't get any."

"Bulllll shit. I got like ten letters coming. Last time I was back at the YRBM I wrote to every fuckin' body I knew."

Morelly moved across the small room to examine

the wall-mounted map of the Vam Co Dong River, which was River Division 435's assignment to patrol. "Seen Mr. Franklin?"

"He's out at the helo pad. Got a civilian coming in who wants to talk to him."

"How far out is the helo?"

"Last I heard he was halfway here from Tay Ninh. So he should be in any sec."

Morelly noted the last contact plotted on the map had been at 0025 the previous night. "Anything in the SPOTREPS on this 0025 contact?"

"Yessir, it's in there. The reports are there on the desk. Shuster and Middleton were killed. Guess you heard about it."

"I didn't get the whole story."

"Yeah. Anyway, their bodies are still out in the box by the Team House."

Morelly frowned as he sat down at the desk across from Post. He leafed through the Spot Reports of recent actions in the Giant Slingshot Operations Area until he found the one he was looking for.

TO: CTF 116
    CTG 194.9
FROM: CTU 194.9.4
INFO: COMUSMACV
       COMNAVFORV
       COMUSARV
       COMRIVRON 43
       COM 5TH SFG, SGN
       CNO, VNN
CONFIDENTIAL
BT

SPOTREP 0340H 25 DEC 68
GIANT SLINGSHOT SPOTREP 189
A. CTU 194.9.4
B. PBRs 711, 713, 717
C. REPORT OF ACTION:
    THREE PBRs IN TRANSIT VAM
    CO DONG RIVER CAME UNDER
    HEAVY AUTOMATIC WEAPONS,
    RIFLE AND ROCKET FIRE TIME
    0025h, 25 DEC 68, COORD XS
    714 590. PBR 711, IN LEAD, RE-
    CEIVED MULTIPLE ROCKET
    HITS. ENGINEER AND BOAT
    SEAMAN LOST OVERBOARD.
    BOAT CAPTAIN KILLED BY
    AUTO WEAPONS FIRE. PBR 713
    AND PBR 717 SLOWED TO AS-
    SIST. PBR 711, TOTALLY DIS-
    ABLED AND IN EXTREMIS,
    TAKEN UNDER TOW BY PBR
    713. BOTH BOATS CLEARED
    KILL ZONE. PBR 717 REMAINED
    BEHIND TO DIVERT HOSTILE
    FIRE AND ATTEMPT RECOVERY
    OF PBR 711 CREWMEN LOST
    OVERBOARD. RECOVERY NOT
    SUCCESSFUL. PATROLS DOWN
    RIVER NOTIFIED TO BE ALERT
    FOR REMAINS. WHILE CLEAR-
    ING KILL ZONE, PBR 717 RE-
    CEIVED ONE ROCKET ROUND,
    PIERCING COXSWAIN'S STA-
    TION, KILLING BOAT CAPTAIN.

ENGINEER TOOK CONTROL
AND PBR 717 CLEARED WITH
PBR 711 AND PBR 713 TO TRA
CU.

D. KIA: MIDDLETON, ROBERT L.,
SM1, USN, B364 687.
AUTO-WEAPONS WOUND TO
HEAD.
KIA: SHUSTER, NEIL L., BM1,
USN, B374 376. MULTIPLE
SHRAPNEL WOUNDS, HEAD
AND BODY.
REMAINS CURRENTLY AT TRA
CU ARMY SPECIAL FORCES
CAMP AWAITING TRANSFER TO
GRAVES   REGISTRATION,
SAIGON.
MIA: TWO. DETAILS TO FOL-
LOW.
WIA: 3 SLIGHT, 1 SERIOUS. PER-
SONNEL CASUALTY REPTS WILL
FOLLOW.

E. REQUEST NOTIFY NEXT OF
KIN, BM1 SHUSTER AND SM1
MIDDLETON

F. OPEN

BT

CONFIDENTIAL

It had been three weeks since the ten Navy PBRs and
sixty-five sailors of River Division 435 had migrated to
the Vam Co Dong River and the desolate American-Viet-
namese Special Forces Camp at Tra Cu.

The operation in which they were engaged was designed to stop the flow of Communist men and war materiel into the Third and Fourth Corps Tactical Zones of South Vietnam from nearby Cambodia, only five kilometers to the west. The Parrot's Beak area of Cambodia, which the Vam Co Dong bordered, had long been known as a Communist stronghold and primary staging area. But for the Viet Cong or North Vietnamese Army—the NVA—to move from the Parrot's Beak to Saigon or into the Mekong Delta, as they had done during the Tet Lunar New Year of 1968, they had to cross either the Vam Co Dong or the Vam Co Tay River. While the former paralleled the Parrot's Beak on the east, the latter bordered it on the south. As these two rivers converged to form the Vam Co prior to emptying into the South China Sea, they geographically resembled a slingshot with one prong on either side of the Parrot's Beak. Hence, the Navy dubbed the campaign Operation Giant Slingshot.

Morelly had missed the first ten days of the operation, being assigned to 435 as a replacement for an officer killed during one of the division's initial firefights. It was getting to the point where becoming a casualty was no longer a novelty.

Morelly whistled lowly to himself as he set the SPOTREP board aside. Twelve hours after the firefight and the remains of both Middleton and Shuster were still in the small metal CONEX storage box. Shuster must have been literally dissected by the shrapnel. And the heat inside the CONEX would have to be up over a hundred. They would be ripe when finally pulled out. Morelly felt a pang of pity, less for Shuster and Middleton than for the helo door gunners who would have to fly with the corpses back to Saigon. "When do you expect someone will be around to fly the bodies out?"

"Damned if I know," Post replied, looking up from his magazine only momentarily. "Mr. Franklin advised Atlantic Island that we have no cold storage capability here. They're trying to con somebody into flying up here later today. I don't know what the fuck they're going to do about 'em, tell you the truth.

"You shoulda been here last night when they brought 'em in, though. Christ, Middleton had, like, no head. Or part of a head. Whatever. Jesus. And Shuster had . . . had holes all over him. Pieces missing. Flak jacket just, like, shreds. He had, like, one boot left and that was it. Then they couldn't find Goddamn body bags for about half an hour so they just laid there on the ground in ponchos outside the door. Goddamn slopes were all crowded around. Probably lookin' to steal the one boot. Shit, they were in bad shape. Finally I just took a bag from the ARVN and, man, we just had to put all the pieces in one bag. Let Saigon sort 'em out, I guess."

One of the tactical radios crackled as someone on the frequency keyed his microphone. "Lansing, Lansing, this is Truckman Three-Two."

Post picked up one of several microphones that lay before him and held it to his mouth. "Roger, Truckman, go ahead."

"Ah, roger, I'm about zero two minutes out of your location at this time. Request marker smoke and advise green deck please." The call sign was unknown to Morelly but he could tell by the vibration-induced vibrato in the caller's voice that he was a helicopter pilot.

"Roger, Truckman. You have a green deck to land on pad west of camp. We'll pop smoke for you. Out. Hey,

Mr. Morelly, can you take the radios for a sec while I run a smoke out to the pad?"

"It's OK, Post," Morelly rose from the desk and reached for one of the smoke grenades that lined the window sill. "I'm qualified to handle it."

"Ha! OK. Hey, give him one of those red ones. We just got 'em in a couple days ago. It's freaking Christmas."

Morelly replaced the grenade marked YELLOW, picked up one of the new ones with the red ring around the top and the word RED stenciled redundantly across the middle and walked out the doorway toward the helo pad. Post began to settle back into his *Dude*, then looked up laughing to himself.

"Hey, Mr. Morelly. That's like fucking Silverman's got on his helmet, right sir?" He yelled after Morelly. "I mean about the gooks. 'Kill 'em all. Let God sort 'em out.' Like that, right Mr. Morelly?" Pause. "Wow. Cute little tits."

THREE

Tra Cu had taken its name and humble beginnings from the abandoned French airstrip that lay to the west of the present camp. Although technically commanded by an Army Captain who was in charge of the U.S. Special Forces "A" Team that resided there, Morelly saw the camp as being run by no one in particular.

There were only two substantial buildings inside the perimeter: the Team House, where the American soldiers lived and ate, and the Operations Center, or NOC, half of which was used by the Vietnamese Special Forces whom the American soldiers were "advising." The Navy's half, Morelly assumed, had at one time been occupied by the Green Berets. When the Navy had moved in, it became incumbent upon the soldiers to give the sailors some kind of space since they offered neither shelter, bedding, cooking facilities nor anything else of any value with the dubious exception of the outhouse.

Aside from the two plaster buildings and the outhouse, Tra Cu was nothing but junk. The helicopter pad divided the camp into two strictly segregated sections of dirty, decaying shacks. One section housed the Vietnamese soldiers and their families, chickens and dogs, while across the pad the Cambodian mercenaries lived in sullen mistrust of both the Americans and the Vietnamese.

On the brighter side of these strained relations, Morelly had seen the most prominent of the Cambodian camp whores and she was stunning in that dark and vaguely defiant way that the Cambodes all seemed to have. At least partly French, he assumed. If the others looked anything like her, that would probably explain why the Cambodian men were seldom seen up and about.

In keeping with the camp's character, the helo pad was no more than a dusty clearing. Nothing out of the ordinary for a remote area of the country that was rarely graced by a visit from the Saigon brass. The cleared pad, resting in the midst of the shacks as it did, became somewhat of a no-man's-land. It formed a natural dividing line between the Vietnamese and Cambodians. Even in the light of day, Morelly had never seen anyone walk across the pad from one side to the other although it was perfectly clear all the way, a distance of about sixty or seventy yards.

As Morelly walked up behind him, Franklin appeared to be concentrating on the empty sky toward the north. Both men were physically similar in features up to a point. Both were rather dark, with dark hair, dark eyes and Asian-tanned skin. Although at 29, Franklin was five years older than Morelly, he looked like he was in his mid-40s. Vietnam had aged Franklin badly. The experience, the responsibility. These things weighed a lot, especially to a good-hearted man like Emmitt Franklin who cared more about his men than about "getting his ticket punched." That was the term used for military lifers who needed a stop in Vietnam, ideally not in direct danger, to round out their service record.

Franklin was cool enough under pressure. Maybe just a little jittery. He always smiled, but it was a nervous smile, like he never trusted anything or anyone. And probably with good reason. He was from the trade school—Annapolis. But Vietnam had made him decide that this would be the end of his Navy career. A leader, he was. A warrior, he wasn't. But then, who was? Few in Vietnam ever wanted to be warriors. It just turned out that way.

Jack Morelly himself was that way. In this land of little people, Morelly was a giant at six feet two inches tall. He considered himself of medium build, weighing over 180 when he had arrived in Vietnam six months earlier. But the stress of operations, and the food, had reduced him by some 20 pounds. Morelly was dark to begin with, but the sun had turned him brown. Frown lines had formed on his gentle forehead and the corners of his eyes showed long hours of anxious vigilance. His straight brown hair had grown long and bleached on the river. His bright blue eyes jumped from his dark face, giving him a look of uncommon intensity not seen this side of a Siberian Husky.

On his right wrist he wore a braided rope bracelet, made by his younger sister, copied meticulously from a manual on seaman's knots. Around his neck was a thin chain of stainless steel, made by his mother to replace the cheap key chain that the armed forces issued for dog tags.

Around one of his two dog tags, Jack had wrapped a piece of once-white adhesive tape. Though his rare and universal blood type, O-RH NEG, was imprinted on his tags, he also wrote it large on the white tape. He felt that if he were killed on the river, the first doctor or medic to reach him would be grateful to know that an immediate source of universal-type blood was at hand to be fed into any surviving comrades.

His goal in life was to be a teacher, as both his father and mother had been, in Connecticut. His dad had died when Jack was only seven, and so his mother had had to quit teaching to, as she put it, "get a real job." With her beauty and her brains, she had become an Administrative Assistant at Xerox in Stamford and worked her way up into the executive ranks. She was now a Vice President of Sales. Very well regarded. Very successful. And she hated every minute of it. Not Xerox. She just missed teaching.

Jack, like his older brother and younger sister, went to UConn, a state school. An English major, Jack fully intended to be a teacher as well. But then Vietnam happened. Jack's dad had served in the Navy in the Pacific in World War II, and had won the Bronze Star Medal for his heroic actions, saving the lives of numerous fellow crewmen when his ship, the destroyer USS Laffey, was attacked by a bunch of kamikazes off of Okinawa.

As much as graduate school and a deferment from the draft appealed to a part of Jack, ducking one's duty, as he saw it, was not in the family, and not in his nature. He enlisted in the Navy and got into Officer Candidate School—eighteen weeks and you're an "officer and a gentleman." Plus $473 a month instead of the $93 that they paid to a Seaman Apprentice. And he remembered asking his dad, just before he died, why he had joined the Navy. "For a clean rack and a warm meal," had been the wry answer. If only dad could see me now, Jack thought . . .

"Merry Christmas, Emmitt?"

"Hey, Jack," Franklin smiled, blinking, after turning

around with a start. "About time you made it. Christ, what'd you do, stop for lunch on the way?"

"No. And you probably didn't save me any either."

"Hell, what for? I was beginning to think you had decided not to come up. You didn't miss us up here at the Tra Cu Hilton?"

"Aw, fuck, we just couldn't get off the barge. Hagren's boat needed a new impeller for one of the pumps and, for sure, it was gonna be in from Nha Be yesterday. Yeah, right. On a fucking sleigh, brought by Santa, right?

"Anyway, so they flew it in at oh-dark-thirty this morning and Hag installed it. Then the fiberglassing on Sturgis's boat hadn't set for some fucking reason. It's OK now, but his boat looks like shit. White holes all over the place 'cause we didn't paint the patches. We'll do that up here tomorrow I guess. Otherwise, here we are . . ."

"Well, that's a long Goddamn story," laughed Franklin. "And what else?"

"Glad you asked. The radar crapped out on the way up. Just like everything else."

"You be able to fix it?"

"Yeah, we'll get it taken care of."

Another laugh. "Well, you're off to a great start. You heard about Shuster and Middleton?"

"I'd heard something about it down at the YRBM. Read the SPOTREP. Post gave me some of the details. Shit, Emmitt, we're getting our ass handed to us up here."

"I know. I know. Well, we're getting our licks in, if that counts for anything. We've got close to 150 Viet Cong and NVA dead so far. We've lost seven now. Saigon likes that . . . a real fine Kill Ratio."

Morelly smiled. "Yeah, I'd like to see one of those fat asses in Washington on the short end of one of those kill ratios. Uhhh . . . here comes the chopper. I gotta pop him some smoke. Where's the wind? Like I can't fucking smell it."

Franklin took off his black beret, the headgear of the Navy's River Patrol Force in Vietnam, and held it up in the air. The two short black ribbons at the back blew slightly eastward toward the camp. As the dot in the air became a distinct shape, Morelly pulled the ring pin on the grenade and threw it toward the pad, downwind of where they stood.

The excited cackle of the Vietnamese women could be heard as the thick red smoke began drifting over the shanties at the edge of the pad. Within seconds, the shack tops were lined with curious spectators, waiting to see the big bird land. Newell watched in renewed amazement as more and more people continued to pile on top of each roof and squat upon a vacant spot. As always, they seemed to appear magically, endlessly, like ants invading a kitchen.

The green Army huey passed about one hundred feet over the pad, then began a slow, descending circle, coming upwind, creating the loud, familiar BAP, BAP, BAP, BAP as its blades, pitched on an angle, beat the air. Franklin hit Morelly's arm and both men began to back away as the helo approached touchdown, nose tilting up in the air. The right-side door gunner leaned out over the skid, one hand on his radio talk button, giving the pilot the distance to the upcoming ground. With lumbering grace, the bird came to rest amidst a torrent of swirling dust. Morelly turned his back on the whole thing. He did not have to see or greet anybody and the dust was becoming a super pain in the ass. He was slightly relieved to hear the dying whistle as the pilot cut his engine. Must be a big shot, he thought. The chopper's going to wait for him.

A small, plump Hispanic-looking man in khaki slacks and white sport shirt hopped from the doorway of the helo and was walking toward them.

"Mr. Mendez, I'm Lieutenant Franklin," Emmitt shouted over the dying rotor blades. Mendez shook his hand and nodded but made no attempt to speak. "This is Lieutenant Morelly, one of my Patrol Officers." This time, just a nod, no handshake. Morelly was slightly annoyed.

Morelly dropped off at the Team House as the other two men strode toward the NOC. The wooden table on one side of the rather large shack had been cleared, giving Morelly a good indication that he had missed lunch. The Army had conceded to feed the patrol officers of 435 provided they pay for it. It was not a bad deal, although Morelly often had some reservations about eating relatively decent food here while he knew the boat crews down at the canal would be getting no better than their choice of picked-over C-rations. So he usually wolfed down a salad here, then went down to the boats and picked at a can of C-ration something.

The wall opposite the dining table featured a crude wooden bar about seven feet in length. Long enough for the Army and 435's officers, but not for the sailors. Morelly walked behind the bar and opened the refrigerator. It was loaded with beer and soft drinks. He picked seven Falstaff cans out, looked in the freezer compartment as an afterthought, replaced the first seven cans and removed seven colder ones from the freezer.

At the going rate of twenty-five cents per can, Morelly owed the Army $1.75. He tore a corner off a well-worn magazine, scribbled out an IOU and dropped it into the empty coffee can under the bar. As he glanced up, his eyes locked onto the shirtless Top Sergeant who had set his *Stars and Stripes* aside and was staring a hole through Morelly's head.

Morelly smiled amiably. "Morning, ah, afternoon, Top."

"Sir."

"You know I'm good for it, right?" He placed two beers in each of his green fatigues' deep thigh pockets. With the remaining three in his hands, he rounded the bar and walked out the doorway, allowing the screen door to slam hard behind him.

As Morelly's enlisted Boat Captain, Boatswain's Mate First Class Walt Hagren, and one of the crewmen approached, Morelly waved a can in the air.

"Boy, can I use one of them bastards," Hagren whistled, patting his hot hairy paunch. "Price," he said to the black man beside him, "how about droppin' this sack of mail in NOC there. Tell Post there's none for him. I'll be down at the boat with Mr. Morelly here."

Engineman Third Class Price Raymond, a tall, skinny, very dark man and a veteran of nearly two years in PBRs, took the bag from Hagren and started off. "How many you got, Mr. Morelly?" He asked, turning around as he walked.

"I got one for you, Raymond, long as you don't let it get warm."

Both Morelly and Hagren ignored the One-Eyed Jack at the gates as he stuck out a bony hand, begging for one of the cans. Morelly wondered for a moment if the man had any idea that the cans were beer. Perhaps he did, but even if he did not, he would beg for one anyway either because he knew he could use it or sell it if it was American, or because begging had simply become his way of life.

Morelly assumed that Hagren would sooner spit in the man's one good eye than give him a can of anything. Hagren was a Boatswain's Mate's Boatswain's Mate. Of medium height, he was considerably overweight by rigid service standards but probably underweight by Boatswain's Mate standards. The Boatswain's Mate job, or rating, was one of the toughest in the Navy. On a ship, the deck and virtually everything that moved on it was the responsibility of the Boatswain's Mate, from muscling the huge anchor windlass on the bow to securing the last thick mooring line on the stern. Being a Boatswain's Mate didn't require all the brains of a Quartermaster (what the Navy called a navigator) or even a Signalman, but it did require common sense, seamanship and the ability to command obedience, if not respect. It was a rating that generally took time in which to advance. But Hagren had moved up from Seaman to Boatswain's Mate Third Class to Boatswain's Mate Second Class in just over two years, on his first ship, a destroyer out of Long Beach. The Navy offered him a promotion to Second Class, however, only if he agreed to ship over for an additional six years. He had done so only in return for orders to Vietnam, which made both him and the Navy happy.

He had gone through the PBR class just after Morelly's at the Inshore Operations Training Center on Mare Island in San Francisco Bay. Four months after arriving in Vietnam, he won a spot promotion to First Class and Franklin gave him his own boat to command, PBR 716. Even in the rugged environment of present operations on the Vam Co Dong, with constant transits back and forth between Tra Cu and the division's permanent base aboard the floating Yard Repair Base Mobile (YRBM) some twenty-five kilometers downstream, Hagren managed to maintain a clean, fast and efficient boat and crew.

Morelly stepped aboard on the bow, walked across the foredeck and down the port gunwale and began passing out his beer. He saved one for Price Raymond and one for himself, giving the remainder to Hagren's other two crewmen, Gunner's Mate Second Class Wayne McGinn and Seaman Don Lemon. Yeoman First Class Sturgis, the lean, bespectacled Boat Captain of Hagren's cover boat moored alongside, came across and became the recipient of the last two cans. He drank one in about five seconds and threw the other across to one of his crewmen.

Having one of his softer lapses into the world he only recently left, Lemon stood leaning against the boat's canopy, sipping his beer and proclaiming the beauties of Christmas in Pennsylvania as opposed to Tra Cu, South Vietnam. With only five patrols under his belt, he was yet to see his first shot fired in anger. Yet, like many young men only eighteen years old, he was anxious to be one of the seasoned corps. Consequently, he always talked a good game, if only for his own benefit. Such reminiscences of home were highly uncharacteristic.

The seasonal lament was broken off quickly, however, as Raymond bounced aboard having presumably delivered the mail into its proper hands. "Well," he cried, stopping midway down the gunwale and peering into the brown water. "Looks like someone here had a good Christmas, man, even if we didn't."

In the current flowing down the canal toward the river, it was not uncommon for trash and garbage to become trapped between two boats moored side by side. Among the empty C-ration boxes, cigarette packages and half-sunken cans, Raymond had spotted a used condom. Hagren never took a moment's notice of the statement, but both Lemon and McGinn moved across the deck to see what Raymond had found so exciting.

"A rubber," Lemon nudged McGinn with a grin, "a damn rubber."

"Yeah, it is," Raymond crooned, stepping onto the engine covers and retrieving his beer from the canopy top. "It is that. And I only wonder who would have the bad manners to use one of them instruments on one of these clean and beautiful young ladies. Hee, hee. I wonder if somebody got that good-lookin' Cambode bitch."

McGinn was an efficient, conscientious nineteen-year-old. He was a tough son-of-a-bitch, but he also laughed a lot. He grew up on a farm in the wheat belt of Kansas, but he'd been around. He quickly recovered from Raymond's discovery and had dismissed the scene, as had everybody else. Except Lemon, who continued to stare at the water.

"Getcha stick, new boy, and you can save it," Raymond laughed.

Lemon quickly straightened up with an angry but slightly whiney, "Aw, fuck you, Raymond."

"Mr. Morelly."

Morelly turned to see Post standing on the mud bank looking anxiously over the boats. "Mr. Morelly, Mr. Franklin wants to see you right away up in NOC, sir."

"Thank you Post." Morelly threw his nearly empty can into the canal. "I'm on my way.

"I'll let you know what's up as soon as I get the word," he called back over his shoulder, receiving a "yessir" from both Hagren and Sturgis.

FOUR

"Post, stand out by the doorway," Franklin said as Morelly entered the NOC. "I don't want any of those gooks in here bothering us for the next few minutes."

"Yessir," Post answered, disappearing, *Dude* in hand. Must have been the year-end Special Issue, Morelly mused. The kid wasn't letting that mag out of his sight for a minute.

Franklin returned immediately to his study of the wall map without acknowledging Morelly's presence. Morelly stood and watched in silence as Franklin and Mendez spoke, the latter pointing occasionally to the map and the former making marks in red grease pencil. This told Morelly something, for every color had a meaning: yellow was used to mark past actions near the river, blue denoted present deployment of 435's boats, and red plotted hot intelligence upon which 435 would act immediately should it be near the river and within the patrol area. From Morelly's vantage point, he could see Franklin making chicken scratches around an area east of the river. In fact, it looked too far to the east to be of concern to the PBRs. Moving a step closer, he saw that the marks were, in fact, on the Vam Co Dong and on the Tan Trang Canal, a narrow, shallow waterway running off the Vam Co Dong to the east.

The Tan Trang Canal was less than three kilometers, or klicks, from the place where Morelly had had his first unhappy experience with 435. North of the Tan Trang Canal, the Vam Co Dong bends like a bow from east to west then back to the east. The division had suffered enough casualties in this area for the sailors to refer to it tritely but validly as "Blood Alley."

It was an ideal ambush site for the Communists because it was close to the safety of Cambodia and they could line up on the west bank without having to cross the river. If they set up on the most western edge of the curving river, they could attack a patrol traveling from the south by first hitting the lead boat head on as it came around the bend. In such a situation, they would enjoy the boats' slow relative motion and thus would have easier targets. Also, of the eight machine guns total aboard two boats in a patrol, only the forward fifty calibers of the lead boat could be brought to bear. As the patrol then swept around the bend, the Viet Cong could pour heavy enfilade fire into both boats. It would only be when the patrol was abreast of the ambush site that the advantage would swing to the boats with their elusive high speed, more experienced gunners and better weapons.

Such an incident had been Morelly's misfortune to experience just shortly after he had joined the division. Well after sundown, Morelly had been aboard Hagren's boat with Sturgis running one hundred yards astern when a large force opened up from the west bank with rockets, automatic weapons and small arms. Hagren had his sailors at battle stations but it still came as a surprise to Morelly. By coincidence, he had been staring intently at the west bank since he knew trouble would come from there if it were to come at all.

Typical in a major ambush, the Communists opened with a series of simultaneously fired, well-aimed rocket rounds. Fortunately, they had waited a few seconds too long. Morelly's boat presented a three-quarter silhouette and was rapidly rounding the bend to a position where all guns could be used.

Morelly gazed in awe as the first rocket, white-hot tail streaming, passed between him in the Coxswain's Flat and Raymond, manning the M-60 light machine gun mounted on the engine covers. Raymond was already returning fire, although it would be another few seconds before he could train his weapon far enough forward to be effective. McGinn in the forward gun tub was pouring rounds out of both fifty-caliber barrels and the boat seaman in the stern, Charnley, was doing the same with his single deck-mounted fifty. Morelly began reaching for the radio mike on the bulkhead in front of him, but he never got to pick it up as a violent explosion bounced him around inside the Coxswain's Flat and threw both primary and secondary microphones to the dark deck.

"Fuckin' engine! They got an engine!" Hagren screamed. "Get on the damn radio!"

Morelly was on all fours, hunting the deck with his hands. "I can't find it!"

Finally grasping one of the mikes, Morelly stood and turned aft, becoming aware of a dying, grinding sound in the stern. Neither Raymond nor Charnley was at his post. It was a second before Morelly realized the stern was under water. Raymond was on his knees, grasping Charnley's flak jacket at the back of the neck, dragging the boy up out of the water onto the higher engine covers.

Morelly reached back over Raymond's shoulder and got his hands on Charnley's left arm. It was slippery and thin in the dark and Morelly realized that the shirt and probably a lot more were gone. Raymond lay back onto the deck as Morelly pulled the body over Raymond's legs and down off the forward edge of the engine covers to the deck area just behind the Coxswain's Flat.

Charnley had not made a sound that Morelly could hear, but because his wounds were apparently caused by shrapnel, Morelly hoped that the flak jacket and helmet had protected the vital areas and kept the body alive.

Still, enough damage anywhere could kill a man and, as he pulled Charnley down to the deck, Morelly noticed the absence of the right foot. A wet black trouser shrouded the leg itself, making it impossible to tell in the dark exactly how far up the amputation had taken place.

Raymond scrambled to his feet once again to man his M-60, but taking one look toward the stern, he jumped off the engine covers, over Charnley's body, and back onto the deck beside Morelly. "We're sinkin', Sir! We're goin' down!"

"I know," Morelly said, picking up the mike again. "Get the kit and see what you can do for Charnley."

Raymond nodded without a word and disappeared below deck to retrieve the first aid kit.

"Victor One, this is Victor," Morelly called into the

mike, trying to hear himself over the incredible din McGinn was causing with his forward fifties. "I took a hit and I'm going down. Get alongside and get us off."

Morelly never heard a signal of recognition from Sturgis in the cover boat behind him. Obviously, Sturgis had known that 716 was in trouble. Even had he not seen the rocket detonation in the stern, he must have nearly overrun Hagren's boat in the darkness as its speed dropped to a crawl with the loss of one of the engines. But whatever the case, Morelly watched gratefully as he saw Sturgis pull out to starboard, increase speed and begin to come alongside.

Morelly looked down at Charnley, being treated at his feet. The rocket had detonated in the stern beneath where Charnley had been standing, firing his machine gun. It had then taken the path of least resistance and blown upward through the fiberglass deck. In the process, it took off one foot, chewed up the other leg and an arm and, it appeared, probably ruined the remainder of Charnley's sex life.

Hagren managed to get the PBR clear of the kill zone just as the one remaining engine choked and drowned itself. Standing in the Coxswain's Flat, the water was now up to Morelly's knees. He had helped Raymond drag Charnley back up onto the engine covers, more exposed to possible gunfire but at least momentarily out of the water. Hagren swore loudly as he pulled both fuel cut-off valves shut to keep diesel fuel from flooding the boat and posing a fire danger.

The boat was resting at nearly a thirty-degree angle with the water line but McGinn, with his guns trained athwartships, never seemed to notice. He had one medal for staying at his post during a firefight on the Mekong

River earlier in his tour. It was a similar situation. The boat he was on could not get out of the kill zone of enemy fire. So as the boat went down, McGinn stayed at his post, in the gun tub, battering away with both barrels. The boat sank stern first and McGinn kept firing as it went. When his mount slipped under water both barrels sizzled, but he still pumped a few more rounds out of them before they jammed dead.

Fortunately, he would not have to do that here. Morelly momentarily lost his balance as Sturgis, being not about to miss the only chance he would have to get alongside, slammed his boat's port bow into 716's starboard side. Once he made contact, he gunned the starboard engine to keep his bow in against the crippled boat. Within seconds, Morelly and Hagren had evacuated the crew, most of whom had managed to salvage a weapon or two. An attempt was made to take the sinking craft in tow, but it faded too fast and was beneath the water before lines could be secured.

McGinn and Raymond had sustained minor wounds in the firefight. Raymond had rescued his M-60 even though it had jammed on him when an AK-47 round had struck the chamber and deflected. Had the round not been stopped, Raymond would almost surely have been killed. As it was, neither he nor McGinn were seriously hurt and they were back on the river the following day. Charnley lost a hand and one leg up to the knee but everything else was saved, including his privates. He was evacuated to Japan and replaced in the crew by Lemon.

Within forty-eight hours, a salvage crew had fought off an assault by an estimated thirty-man NVA force to successfully raise PBR 716 and tow her out of the area. Returned down river to the YRBM-14, she was repaired and refitted in four days of round-the-clock maintenance. A week after she had been sunk, she was ready to fight again.

"Jack, what do you think?"

"Sorry, Emmitt. What's that?"

"I said, 'Do you think you can get up the Tan Trang Canal with a PBR?'"

"I don't know, Emmitt. It's only been done before in airboats. High tide is sometime tomorrow morning. We maybe could make it then."

"Well, I'm afraid you might have a chance to be the first to give it a try, old buddy."

"Sounds great," Morelly answered weakly. His palms began to sweat more than they already were and he burped up some of his Falstaff.

"Mr. Mendez," Franklin turned toward the dark, heavy man. "Mr. Morelly here will be in command of any patrol we might run up the Tan Trang or any other canal off the Vam Co Dong, so why don't you go over this thing again, slowly, for both of us."

Franklin lit a Winston and sat down at his desk while Morelly lit what was for him the first Marlboro of the day.

Mendez began in a low monotone without any trace of any form of accent. "We were contacted a while ago by a sometime agent of ours in the Tay Ninh City area, north of here. He is known by us to work occasionally with the local VC in that area. The VC know in turn that he has on occasion spoken to our people in both Tay Ninh and Go Dau Ha. He remains more or less neutral and since the VC to whom the nature of his actions is known are somewhat less loyal to their cause than to the American dollar, they allow him to survive." Mendez reached into his pocket for a cigarette. Morelly lit it for him.

"He has assisted us in the past when we have seen fit to meet his price. Generally his help has been in the nature of intelligence, often good intelligence. Very good. The area around Tay Ninh and Go Dau Ha, as you know, lies in the heart of a prime infiltration corridor for North Vietnamese regulars moving from Cambodia toward Saigon or on toward Delta cities such as Vinh Long, Ben Tre or My Tho. These local VC I spoke about are often alerted to expect and aid NVA troops when they pass through. For a price, the locals will occasionally pass the word of such an infiltration to us via our friend. We have caught a lot of movement and gotten some good body count this way.

"This time, however, the offer involves an American prisoner that the locals claim to hold. They say he is an Army Light Observation Helicopter pilot shot down near the Parrot's Beak about two weeks ago. This checks out with the Army, but of course that doesn't prove anything. When I met with our agent a few days ago, I made this clear to him but maintained that we would be interested if he or his comrades could prove the man was, in fact, alive and their prisoner.

"According to this guy, an NVA unit moving out of the Plain of Reeds toward Saigon captured the pilot. They kept the man alive only because he was not wounded and did not slow them down. If he had, of course, they would have killed him. At any rate, the NVA passing through delivered him into the hands of our enterprising VC for safekeeping when they arrived in Tay Ninh. He's not in the city, I'm afraid. He's being held in the boonies someplace pending our friend's success or failure at making a deal with us. Now our man did hint, when I talked with him, that the pilot was somewhere south of Go Dau Ha, which brings it into your Op Area, I believe."

"And if you can make a deal with this guy, you want our boats to get the pilot out, right?" Morelly asked, hoping he was wrong but knowing he was not.

"Yes, that's it," Mendez nodded, crushing out his butt. "First we will have to make contact with our man. That has been arranged. The meeting will take place aboard one of your PBRs in the river off the Hiep Hoa sugar mill at five o'clock tomorrow morning. I will be on your boat. Unfortunately, you cannot take two boats to the area, as I understand you generally would. Once the pickup of our friend is made, your boat will cruise up and down the river at slow speed in front of Hiep Hoa until we determine if he and I can settle on a satisfactory arrangement."

Morelly glanced at Franklin and drew a sympathetic nod and an immediate reaction. "Mr. Mendez, we simply do not operate with a single boat. This river is narrow and packed with VC. If a boat is hit and sunk or disabled, its crew is as good as dead if there isn't a covering boat nearby to assist."

"Yes, I can fully appreciate your situation. I realize that it is your cardinal rule of survival to always operate in pairs, since your boats are highly vulnerable and are the only means you have of getting out of a bad spot. I can understand your feelings, but if there is a chance to pick up a prisoner, especially an American, we must take the chance, even if it is on Charlie's terms.

"Unfortunately our agent, while cooperative, is somewhat less than trusting and has promised not to appear if he feels there is too much force present at the sugar mill.

Ah . . . should you need to obtain higher authority in order to permit a single boat to proceed independently, I have earlier visited with Lieutenant Commander Getzel, your Squadron Commander, regarding this operation. I am certain he will support my feeling that we have no choice, really, but to do all we can to rescue this pilot should he be alive."

Franklin exploded. "You went and saw Getzel on the YRBM before I knew anything about this Goddamn thing?"

"I was flying from Saigon to Go Dau Ha earlier today and just thought that while I was about it I might stop and clear things with him. Save you the trouble."

"Well thanks a fucking bunch. That's certainly appreciated."

"Yes, well, now with the one boat we will try and make a deal with our contact on board. We must pick him up precisely at five since he will be waiting for us then but does not wish to remain exposed for any length of time. Especially since five is the end of curfew. He wouldn't want the wrong people to see him getting willingly onto an American patrol boat then cruising offshore for awhile.

"I will have with me the sum of 200,000 piasters. If he proves to my satisfaction that the pilot is in their possession, I will give him the money and he will, in return, give me directions to the pickup point. Now understand that the pickup may be immediately following the meeting or it may be set for another day, for all I know. We'll have to be prepared to make it tomorrow morning just in case. And the agreement is one boat all the way. That means if the prisoner grab is to be, as I suspect, up one of the canals off the Vam Co Dong, probably the Tan Trang, only one boat will be able to make the run. At the point of the grab, you may have to use some tracer fire into the air to direct the pilot to the boat through the underbrush."

"We'll have the Seawolves on alert the entire morning," Franklin said, hoping to allay some of Morelly's fears. "And most of those canals are in Free Fire Zones. The Tan Trang is a twenty-four-hour Free Fire from just off the Vam Co Dong all the way up to Tan Trang Village."

"We should have no trouble from the agent or the local VC with whom we may deal," Mendez continued. "200,000 piasters is a large sum and they would probably want to keep their part of the bargain so that we could one day deal again. The only threat will be that if we are forced to transit far up a tributary or canal, we will be fair game for anyone else. The sound of PBR engines is like nothing the Vietnamese would have. Any North Vietnamese unit possibly in the area will know it must be an enemy. Whether they feel it's worthwhile to hit us, if in fact they are in the area, no one knows. It certainly could happen."

"Why do you feel you need a PBR for this operation?" Morelly asked. "Couldn't you get an Army ground patrol from the MACV advisory compound up at Go Dau Ha to go with you?"

Mendez appeared to be straining to hear. Morelly realized that he had been mumbling as though he was really asking himself the question. "I would rather take an Army combat patrol myself. I wouldn't feel so naked. I don't at all see how you people justify running around in those little green boats in the first place. But, as I told you, these people are very conscious of a trick. Like all

VC, they have an intense fear of American firepower.
For this reason, they would never accept a ground patrol.
They would be at a tactical disadvantage if their plans
were to go wrong. Obviously, they wouldn't go for a
helo pickup either. That to them is asking to be struck
by lightning. And certainly I'm not going to walk in there
by myself."

Morelly nodded his acceptance of Mendez' explanation. The rationale fit his general opinion of the Oriental
mind. Somehow he felt that the Communists did not
so much mind being killed so long as it was in relatively
lesser numbers than the Americans. He removed another
Marlboro from the plastic watertight box he kept in his
left thigh pocket and lit it off the butt he had just finished. "Where are you going to be, Mr. Mendez? I mean,
will you be here or will we pick you up somewhere tonight or tomorrow?"

"I will return shortly to the MACV compound at
Go Dau Ha to work out a few more details which will
not concern the Navy. You know the landing just north
of the waterfront fish market?"

Morelly nodded, staring through his burning cigarette ash. He knew the area between Tra Cu and Go Dau
Ha like the proverbial back of his hand. Twenty klicks of
twisting, unpredictable territory.

"Good. Then why don't you pick me up there at,
say, four and that should give us plenty of time to get to
the sugar mill by five." Mendez realized that Morelly
was not about to answer, so he turned to Franklin for
approval.

"That'll be OK with us."

"I'm going to leave here and go up river with two
boats," Morelly said, speaking his thoughts aloud. "To

transit up to Go Dau Ha to pick you up, there's no reason why we should make the trip alone. Then if you
want, I'll have my cover boat stay there."

"I have no objection to that, Mr. Morelly. I will leave
you gentlemen to work out the details on your end.
Thank you, Emmitt," he said, using Franklin's first name
for the first time. They shook hands. "I know my way to
the pad. We'll see you tomorrow morning, Mr. Morelly."

"Bright and early."

"Fine." And the big hulk was out the doorway.

"Post," Morelly called. "Go get Hagren and Sturgis
and tell them I'd like to see them ASAP."

A quick "yessir" resounded from outside the doorway and Morelly glanced out the room's lone window
to see Post walk rapidly through the dust toward the
canal.

"Looks like you and Mendez are well on your way
to establishing a long and lasting friendship," Franklin
mused.

Morelly smiled weakly, not at all looking forward to
an experience such as this one with a character whom he
instinctively did not like much. "I don't know about that
cruising around off Hiep Hoa, among other things," he
said, changing the subject.

Franklin nodded. "I know what you mean."

And he did. Hiep Hoa was about seven kilometers
north of Tra Cu. From the time 435 had begun patrolling the Vam Co Dong River, Hiep Hoa had been considered a "friendly" area, under government control. During the day, PBRs had frequently gone into the village
marketplace to purchase black-market Coke and beer and
to get large blocks of ice that they would chip down and
pack into the boats' small Igloo water coolers. In an ef-

fort to "win the hearts and minds of the people," as the psychological warfare dictum demanded, the boats had always slowed to idle speed when passing through the village to avoid swamping the sampans and homes at the river's edge.

At dusk one night, just a few days prior to Morelly's incident along Blood Alley, Franklin was out commanding a patrol himself, as he generally did once or twice a week. His two boats were running at idle speed through Hiep Hoa when a Viet Cong force dug in on the west bank opened fire with rockets and small arms. The patrol had somehow managed to clear the area with only one casualty: a rocket had struck the forward superstructure just aft of the fifty-caliber mount. Part of the blast had penetrated below decks, causing only minor damage, but a large portion of the shrapnel had blown forward. The forward gunner had trained his fifties to port and was commencing fire when this shrapnel hit him full in the left side of the head. He would have died instantly were it not for his steel helmet. As it was, most of the left side of his face was blown away, his jaw was left hanging agape and his left eye was missing. He lived long enough to be placed aboard an Air Force Pedro medical evacuation helicopter, but there was nothing the paramedic on board could do for him and he died before reaching the 24th Evacuation Hospital down river at Binh Thuy.

Franklin had been standing in the Flat next to the Coxswain when the explosion occurred and the flash had temporarily blinded both men. Still, the Coxswain managed to steer on some form of miraculous instinct until his sight returned seconds later. The patrol made it safely to Go Dau Ha where the Pedro had touched down to take the dying sailor off.

With Franklin's boat damaged and unable to retaliate, he radioed Chief McAndles, a conservative Patrol Officer who rarely took chances and was thus very popular with some sailors and very unpopular with others. He had only forty-some days left in Vietnam out of an extended tour of eighteen months. Receiving word of the action, he scrambled two boats from Tra Cu and ran full bore through Hiep Hoa, putting all the ordnance he had on the west bank. Clearing the area, he called in artillery fire on the line of grass shacks, or "hootches," requesting white phosphorous rounds that would incinerate anything near the point of detonation. After twenty minutes of shelling, he took his boats back into the area.

Tying a rag on the end of a long boat hook and dipping it in diesel fuel, he led a small party ashore and proceeded to burn all remaining structures to the ground. In the eerie glow of crackling yellow flames, a grimly satisfied boat crew pulled back out to midstream and headed south to Tra Cu, content in the knowledge that they had evened the score while the iron was still hot. Had they known that the wounded machine gunner had died en route to the hospital, the east bank of the village could well have been razed also.

Although the incident had taken place quite some time ago, a yellow circle with date-time group designation still marked the Hiep Hoa area on the map.

Morelly now noted a red date-time group "261255H" around the Tan Trang Canal, just north of Hiep Hoa. The day being December 26, slightly after 1300 in the afternoon, Morelly correctly assumed that these were the marks Franklin had made earlier while talking with Mendez.

FIVE

With a loud clump of heavy boots, Hagren strode through the doorway, followed by Sturgis and Post. "Yessir," Hagren croaked, pulling his loose-fitting trousers up over his belly.

"Want to give you people a briefing, Hagren," Franklin said. "Oh, first . . . Post, get on the radio to Atlantic Island and tell them to have the Swing Helo stop here this afternoon and pick me up." He glanced at Morelly. "I want to talk to that Goddamn Commander Getzel about this thing. I should be back around supper."

Morelly nodded along with Post's "yessir" and the latter immediately keyed one of his microphones and began the preliminary exchange of call signs. Franklin stepped up to the map as Hagren and Sturgis moved forward in anticipation.

"We just had a visit from a MACV intelligence type from the Tay Ninh-Go Dau Ha area. The Army wants us to run an op tomorrow morning early. Possibly up the Tan Trang or one of the other canals off the river. The object will be to pick up an American pilot held prisoner, we think, by the VC or NVA."

Sturgis said nothing, not moving an eye from the map. Hagren turned his head slowly from the map to Morelly to Franklin and back to the map. His baggy bloodhound eyes said nothing.

"Mr. Morelly and I will work out the details. You won't be going out today as scheduled since you'll be up a good part of the night. Right now, I'd say plan to get underway at oh-three-hundred tomorrow morning since you'll need to be up at Go Dau Ha by four."

"Should we put on extra ammo or anything?" Hagren asked, turning to Morelly.

"How many rounds are you each carrying now?" Morelly had not the slightest idea what the answer might be. He knew what the River Patrol Force prescribed in its manuals, but he also knew that since moving to the Vam Co Dong all the boats were carrying more than the permitted ammo loads.

"I've got about 3,000 rounds of fifty, 1,500 rounds of seven-point-six two and two belts of forty millimeter. Plus a case of concussion grenades, some M-79 rounds, the twelve-gauge and maybe ten or fifteen M-16 magazines," Hagren answered, looking down the last page of a small black notebook he had drawn from his breast pocket.

Sturgis nodded. "I've got about the same, but only 2,500 rounds of fifty."

"For reasons that we don't need to go into right now, it looks like this will be a two-boat operation only part of the way," Morelly continued. "We'll first transit to

Go Dau Ha, pick up an intelligence man, and proceed back down river. I'll be on 716 and Sturgis, you'll follow at about a hundred yards.

"Emmitt, I thought about leaving 714 off at Go Dau Ha, but do you see any reason why Sturgis can't follow us back down river? Then when we drop off around the sugar mill at Hiep Hoa, he can keep going back here to Tra Cu."

"No, I think the original idea is better. If anything happens at Hiep Hoa, Sturgis would only be seven klicks away here at Tra Cu. But I think we should bet that if you're going to have trouble, it's going to be with the pickup of the pilot. Since we are reasonably sure that that pickup will be further up river, between Hiep Hoa and Go Dau Ha, I think it would be best to have Sturgis standing by at Go Dau Ha like we originally planned. I'll send a message down to the YRBM to have one of the Chiefs get a couple of boats underway for here as soon as possible, so you'll have a quick reaction force here too by the time you get underway."

Morelly nodded at Franklin's forethought and obvious concern. "OK, that sounds great. Sturgis, then you'll drop off at Go Dau Ha and stand by the radios for the rest of the morning. At least until it's over. Hag, since we'll be going on, possibly to make the pickup, I think some extra ammo would be good to have."

Morelly and Hagren proceeded to agree on 3,000 rounds for the twin fifties mounted in the metal scarf ring on the fore deck and 1,000 rounds for the can that fed the deck-mounted single fifty in the stern. An extra can of 1,500 rounds of linked 7.62 ammunition for the M-60 light machine gun would be added to the 1,500-round can already on board. For the forty-millimeter grenade launcher, or Honeywell as it was called after its manufacturer, they decided that two belts or eighty rounds would be sufficient.

In addition to this paraphernalia, Hagren was to secure additional M-16 automatic rifle magazines, as many high explosives and illumination rounds as he could get for the single-shot M-79 grenade launchers, and two extra flak jackets and helmets, one for Mendez and one for the pilot.

"Any questions?" Morelly asked warily.

"If you get into it with just one boat," Sturgis said, "well, I never heard of anybody being out without a cover boat before. But shit," he added with a slight smile and a shrug, "what can you do, I guess." He was questioning neither Morelly nor Franklin. Ideas such as this one simply had to be accepted as facts of life in a war like Vietnam. Most of these brainstorms were assumed to come from a higher echelon of command where the men who gave the orders rarely had to endure the consequences.

"Once you have the intelligence man on board," Franklin said quietly, "you'll be looking for a VC informer." He had obviously felt that he owed Hagren and his crew at least some further explanation. "The guy has been used before by the Army, apparently always with good results. The idea will be to get him on board your boat and have the spook make a deal with him. This spook—Mendez is his name—is with USAid. Probably CIA. Anyway, he insists that one and only one PBR come and get him. And the feeling is that under the circumstances a calculated risk such as this is worth taking."

Sturgis let out a long low whistle. Hagren glanced around and smiled mockingly. "Fuckin' Navy's all right, boy. It's allfuckingright." Then, changing the subject as though it had never entered his head, he asked about getting underway.

"Tell the radioman when you want to get up. Like Mr. Franklin suggested, we'll leave at three."

"How about let's get the frequencies and all straight now," Morelly asked after Hagren and Sturgis had left. Franklin began to speak as Morelly drew out his notebook.

"OK. 45.10 is your primary circuit. Use it for the standard tactical transmissions only, just the normal stuff. Put your secondary on 55.05. That'll be your Secure. Use your regular call sign, Lansing Victor. Mendez gave me one coded message he will send or he wants you to send if and when a pickup of the pilot is made. You'll call in 'Bright Knight has landed with one man from the moon'." Morelly felt this to be an apt if somewhat less than totally original bit of cloak and dagger. The Apollo 10 astronauts were at that very minute whirling around the moon.

"As I said, the Seawolf Fire Team down on the YRBM will be on standby for a Scramble One until you get back. If you want them, call me and I'll relay. The flight should have Seawolf Five One flying Fire Team Lead." Huey helicopter gunships, on loan to the Navy from the Army, were the river sailors' guardian angels. Nicknamed "Seawolves," the gunships operated in teams of two. Based as close as possible to the center of a riverine operation, their main function was to support Navy boats in trouble. More than a few times, Seawolves had saved the men on 435's boats, sometimes with heavy suppressive firepower, sometimes by dropping needed ammunition or supplies. And sometimes by being on the spot before a medical evacuation helicopter could begin to respond to a call for help.

Whether such support would be called for in the next twenty-four hours, Morelly did not know or even care to guess. He was grateful that the help would be available, however. With this satisfaction and the image of a bright knight landing on the moon, he left the crackling radios and made his way past the Team House to the plywood and tin supply shack where both the Special Forces team and the River Division kept spare parts, ammunition and toilet paper. Coincidentally, it was also the Patrol Officers' bunkroom.

Since no more than four Patrol Officers were expected to be asleep at the camp at any one time, there were only four racks set up—pea green canvas and wood Army cots. Two of them boasted mosquito netting and were thus the most coveted. No one claimed any particular rack as his own on a permanent basis. A man simply fell into the closest empty space after entering the door. Most of the senior enlisted men who were Patrol Officers—the old Chiefs Petty Officers in the division— were not too choosy about where they slept or what they slept in. Consequently, they never bothered to pull the filthy sheets off the cots and throw them out the door for a Vietnamese mama-san to launder. Most of the cots stunk, as did the pillowcases. Morelly could hack the dirty sheets when he was tired enough, but a pillowcase was something else. Thus, his habit was to take off his fatigue shirt, lay the pillow inside it, and button up the shirt. The result was a headless, legless dummy upon whose stomach Morelly always slept.

He also preferred the racks with the mosquito netting over the top and around the sides. The Chiefs claimed that the bugs did not bite inside the shack at night and Morelly felt a bit less than rugged arguing that point with them. In fact, the real reason he wanted a cot with a net was so that he could feel secure from the rats that patrolled the shack from dark to dawn. When he had first arrived at Tra Cu, during his second night in the camp, he had lain down to sleep on one of the unprotected cots against the wooden wall. Exhausted from an all-day patrol, he had removed his shirt and trousers but lacked the energy to pull of his wool socks. He reflected later that that had been a fortunate omission, for in the middle of the night a tickling of his right foot awakened him. When a few tired wriggles of his toes failed to stop the tickling, Morelly started up in bed, wide awake, realizing that he was being eaten.

Seizing the flashlight, which he always kept at hand, he shone it down to the foot of the cot. There, over the top of a big toe which was exposed through a small hole in the wool, he focused on the glint of two frightened beady eyes. It then became a question of who moved faster to get away from whom. The feet went one way, the hungry rodent the other. Morelly was left shuddering in the night, wondering what would have happened if the sock had not been there. He got no more sleep that night although he did do a lot of listening.

Removing his boots now, Morelly crawled under the nearest mosquito netting and stretched out. The ceaseless banter of the women, dogs and children outside vied with thoughts of the coming operation until he fell asleep.

SIX

Headquarters, On-Scene Commander
Operation Giant Slingshot
Yard Repair Base (Mobile)-14
Vam Co River, Republic of Vietnam

Franklin was out of the helo and moving down the ladder from the flight deck almost before the aircraft landed.

As he pushed through the heavy watertight door into the YRBM-14's Officer Country, he was greeted by the cold blast of air conditioning that chilled the sweat against his body and made him shiver. Although he maintained a stateroom on board, he had not slept in it since the Giant Slingshot campaign had begun earlier in December. While the cool air made him uncomfortable now, he could not forget the luxury of being in Vietnam and still sleeping under two blankets to keep the chill out.

Passing the Wardroom, he poked his head through

the door to find only a single steward setting places at the table.

"Hey, Mr. Franklin," the Filipino grinned, "where you be so long? You want me set a place for you for tonight?"

"No, thank you, Nacional. Have you seen Commander Getzel around?"

"He's in here a while ago to have me make him some fresh coffee. You want some fresh coffee?"

"No, thank you."

Although the food at Tra Cu was often drab and tasteless, it was at least nourishing. Far more so, it seemed, than what the YRBM-14 had to offer: a variety of over-cooked meats and vegetables with instant mashed potatoes and vanilla ice cream that had been melted and re-frozen more than a few times.

Walking aft from the wardroom, Franklin stopped at the door bearing a neatly lettered walnut plaque:

Ray S. Getzel
Lieutenant Commander, U.S. Navy
Commander, River Squadron 43
And underneath, a hand-stenciled cardboard sign:
On-Scene Commander
Operation Giant Slingshot

Franklin knocked, entered and stood face-to-face with his boss, whom he despised.

As usual, Getzel appeared to have just emerged from an overall body manicure. He was a slight little man, somewhat less than five feet six who, Franklin guessed, attempted to compensate for his size by being exquis-itely neat and well scrubbed. Even in the few instances where Franklin had known the man to exert himself physically, not a hair ever slipped out of place. Since he spoke with a hint of a lisp, Morelly frequently permitted himself the luxury of openly speculating, always to Franklin's riotous laughter, what could conceivably transpire should Getzel ever catch another officer alone in the head, in the dark, from the back.

"Well, Emmitt," Getzel said, looking up from his desk, "I had no idea you were back on board."

"I just came in on the Swing Ship. I'll be going back on the return trip in about an hour or so. I wanted to talk to you about this Army intelligence guy or whatever he is."

"Mr. Mendez?"

"Yes, Mendez."

"He's U.S. Information Agency. At least that's what he said he was."

"I doubt that. Anyway, he's a spook. CIA, I'm guessing. But I want to know about this operation that was agreed upon before I knew anything about it."

"Now hold on, Emmitt. It was probably coincidental that Mr. Mendez was flying from USAid in Saigon to Go Dau Ha or Tay Ninh or someplace. He decided to kill two birds with one stone and just stop in and get my reaction to this operation. Emmitt, we did not agree to carry this thing out, if that's what you think. I would not presume to commit your boats to any operation without first checking with you. You know that. You're the Division Commander and only you can run those boats."

"Commander, we're getting killed up there just running the river itself. There must be thousands of gooks swarming around the Parrot's Beak, all trying to get past us and the Army and get to Saigon or the Delta in time for Tet. In the past twenty days since we started Sling-shot I've lost two boats and about a dozen men dead or medevacked. I've got fifty-one men as of this morning and at least twenty-five of them have already been wounded once and returned to duty."

"I realize what your statistics are, Emmitt. Who do you think has to answer to the Commodore for every lost man or boat? Christ, I thought he'd have a Goddamn stroke when 716 was sunk and we didn't have it back on the line within forty-eight hours."

"And now we're talking about sending a boat off the river and up a canal all by itself? That Tan Trang Canal is barely wide enough to turn around. A PBR can only run it when the water's up. If we get caught up there, it'll be a mess."

"Yes, Emmitt, but look at the objective. An American prisoner. An American, Emmitt. God almighty, we can't leave him in the hands of the Communists if there's even the slightest chance of him being rescued."

"If it costs us five men and a boat?"

"Emmitt, look. Jesus Christ. I spoke with the boss—with the Commodore—earlier today regarding this operation. Don't think I take this whole thing lightly and, needless to say, Captain McGinnis doesn't either. I described the situation to him as best I could. Certainly he is aware of what's been transpiring along the Vam Co Dong since December sixth. Just a moment."

Getzel pulled himself up to the desk and began sorting through a file of papers until he found a list of figures and studied it momentarily.

"Why, Emmitt, do you know that 435 has had by far and away the most success on Giant Slingshot of any of the six divisions we have up there, either on the Vam

Co Dong or the Vam Co Tay? Why look here . . . 146 kills—and that's by body count—and God knows how many more you killed that the little bastards dragged away. I believe the next closest division is 551 but they have only 98.

"And your Kill Ratio! Let's see . . . 146 gooks against, what have you lost, dead? Seven so far? Emmitt, man, that's like 20-to-1. That's beyond acceptable, as you know. You should be very proud of that statistic. And my God, Emmitt, you people have gotten nearly all the decent-size arms caches we've had on Slingshot.

"Well," he concluded, sighing weightily as he dropped the fact sheet back onto the pile. "What I'm getting at here, Emmitt, is that both the Commodore and I have confidence in your decision on this thing. You've done a hell of a job in a mighty bad area. It's a job that wouldn't have gotten done if we didn't have an aggressive man like you up there running the show. That's why the Commodore naturally felt you would leap at this chance to expand your operations and pull off, well, something of a coup at the same time.

"You know our relations with the Army up there have not been the greatest. And believe me, Emmitt, when the Third Corps General in Can Tho puts the heat on Admiral White down there to have us either cooperate or move out, the impact is felt by the Commodore and then on down to me. So on that count, I don't need to tell you what something like pulling out an Army man could do for our relations.

"At any rate, Emmitt, whatever you decide, give your crew a 'good luck' for me. I know you people can pull it off. At our end here, we'll be waiting for progress reports and of course we'll have the Seawolves standing by to scramble if there's trouble. O.K.?"

"Yessir." Getzel had closed the discussion. Further talk would be futile. The non-order order, Franklin thought. Getzel's covered and we're set up to be left out to dry.

Getzel stood and walked around the desk to show Franklin out. "And hell, Emmitt, when are you going to be getting back here for a rest? You've been up at that damn camp since before Slingshot began, haven't you? Why your damn martini gizmo is getting cobwebs on the stirrer."

"I don't know, Commander. Maybe I'll get the Exec up there to relieve me for a couple of days next week."

"Great. Fine. Well, have a good flight back and don't forget to give my best to the men."

"Yes, sir."

SEVEN

Advanced Tactical Support Base
Tra Cu

Morelly had finally dozed off when Post tapped him on the shoulder to tell him he didn't want him to miss dinner, implying gaily that there was a possibility that it would be his last.

Such morbid humor, Morelly believed, was a natural defense mechanism employed by men in danger. While he did not consciously subscribe to it, he caught himself using it occasionally in an attempt to divert his mind's attention from the tight, sick butterfly feeling that frequently gripped his guts. He only frowned slightly at Post as he stumbled off the cot. It was nearly dusk and Morelly glanced back at the sinking sun as he strode toward the Team House, buttoning up his fatigue shirt, which had once again served him well as a pillowcase.

As usual, he found supper a culinary disaster. The

day's earlier look of disbelief on the face of the Top Ser-
geant had now turned into one of full distaste as he
glanced occasionally at Morelly, making it obvious that
the ramifications of removing seven beers at one time
from the rationed refrigerator had finally hit home.

In an effort to avoid the Top, Morelly sat at the far
end of the rather long table. There was room for six on
either side but, as it was, four soldiers sat at one end
while Morelly sat at the other. This situation he did not
mind except for the fact that the tray of fresh cucum-
bers, tomatoes, shallots and French bread was at the Army
end. Generally, Morelly made an entire meal of these
delights since the main course was usually sub-par to say
the least. The Vietnamese could raise delectable vegetables
and the French had taught them well in the art of bread
making. Fortunately, the night's pork was edible, so
Morelly did not feel the necessity of demeaning himself
by sliding down the bench to raid the tray.

However, immediately following the meal he did
feel compelled to visit the outhouse. There he sat, alone
with his thoughts, as through the waist-high wire fly screen
he watched the Vietnamese sun sink slowly toward the
sloping Cambodian mountains in the distance. A beautiful picture. Such a crummy place. His right foot puffed
a beat in the lime powder that had been spilled on the
wooden floor and he whistled idly to himself.

Reflecting momentarily as he bent over the stained
wooden hole to retrieve a sodden role of toilet paper, he
decided that he should have partaken of the green vegetables after all. This thought he dismissed, however, as
he received a dose of lime dust in his eyes while dumping
a cupful of the fine, powdery substance into the hole on
top of his contribution. He blinked, sniffed wetly and

sneezed as he pushed his way back through the doorway. He replaced the padlock on the hinge and returned the key to its hook in the Team House.

Morelly had at one time wondered why a lock was needed on a seemingly little coveted piece of property such as the head. He wondered until one day he had walked in and found that someone had left it unlocked. As he opened the door he was greeted by the sheepish grin of a middle age Vietnamese woman. Her well-worn pajama top she had pulled up to the middle of her back as she held the excess material bunched up beneath her sagging breasts. The bottoms were rumpled around her ankles. She was not sitting, however. Instead, she was squatting, on top of the seat, one foot on either side of the egg-shaped hole. Her knees were thrust straight up to her chin and her arms wrapped around her shins. The scene made him slightly nauseous, especially when he saw that the naked brown buttocks were positioned too far aft of the hole. She was depositing a snaky load on the back of the seat.

"Get the fuck out of here, *Co!*" He shouted.

The woman's sheepish grin faded immediately, to be replaced by a look of sheer terror. She began to jabber rapidly toward the screen. She was apparently calling for assistance, but none arrived, everyone being afraid to tamper with what was obviously one of the Americans' most treasured possessions. Not even NOC or the Team House was locked except in the middle of the night.

"Get the fuck out of here!" Morelly screamed again. Understanding the threat if not the words, she hopped off the seat onto the floor. Pulling the bottoms up to her breasts and letting the top fall over her bulging stomach, she dashed past Morelly and out the doorway. Reaching the hootches nearby, she was greeted by frowning women and grinning men. One of the latter waved at Morelly, pointed to the woman and pounded the fist of his right hand in the palm of his left in the well-known gesture that a Vietnamese man or boy used when offering the services of one of his women to a GI.

Morelly still wondered, on occasion, who had cleaned up the woman's mess. He hadn't.

"Post," Morelly said, stepping into NOC. "Get me up at oh-two-hundred, will you? Anything going on?"

"No, sir. Yessir, I'll get you up at two. That is I'll leave word for the next watch to get you up. Mr. Franklin's back from Atlantic Island. Got back while you were eating, I guess."

"He ask to see me?"

"No, sir."

Morelly noticed the dog-eared *Dude* lying unattended on top of one of the radios. Post was now devouring a novel, obviously a classic, and had barely looked up when Morelly walked through the doorway. Now he was again concentrating deeply. Morelly stood looking down for a moment whereupon Post, feeling the eyes on him, looked up and tilted the paperback against his chest so Morelly could see the cover: *Lust Lovers*.

"Pretty good?"

"Yeah, but Vince's got it after me. You can ask him if anyone's got it after him."

Morelly smiled, shook his head, and departed for the supply shack and a few more hours among the rats.

EIGHT

The red-lensed flashlight flared into Morelly's closed eyes. As he opened them, the red light splashed blood-like on the back of his brain.

"Mr. Morelly, hey, wake up. Mr. Franklin wants see you. Right now. Mr. Morelly, you up?"

"Goddamn it, Post, get that fucking light out of my Goddamn eyes! Jesus Christ! I can't see shit. God DAMN it!"

"Sorry sir. I wanted to make sure you were up. You want me to help you?"

"No, no. I've got a light here somewhere. Tell Mr. Franklin I'll be right there. Hey, Post, it's only five after twelve."

"I know sir. But Mr. Franklin just took a message on Secure from Country Store at Go Dau Ha and said to get you right away."

Morelly threw his legs out onto the floor, then picked them up quickly. Sitting cross-legged on the cot, he reached over for the flashlight he kept in his right boot and flashed it around the shack. This done, he quietly set his feet back onto the floor and began to lace up his boots. He'd be glad when he got home and didn't have to worry about the Goddamn rats amputating his Goddamn toes.

Franklin was making a notation in red on the wall map as Morelly entered. Post sat quietly at his radios, likely irritated by the fact that it was after midnight and he had not yet been relieved. Hagren lounged at Franklin's desk, hunching half awake over the cup of coffee that sat between his huge hands. Sturgis leaned against the filing cabinet behind Hagren's chair.

"Coffee there, sir," Post looked up, pointing to a steaming cup resting on top of the nearest radio.

"Thanks."

"I just talked to Mendez on Secure, Jack." Franklin began.

"How'd he get our Secure key?" Morelly sunk to the wooden bench beside the wall map. All Secure radios had to be reset every day at midnight by repositioning a number of small devices within each set according to a secret key list.

Although both the Army and the Navy operated together on the Vam Co Dong, neither had seen fit (or perhaps trusted the other well enough) to offer to exchange keys or employ a single key between them. Consequently, all classified messages between Army and Navy had to be coded word-by-word for transmission via regular radio channels.

"He called two of the 551 boats on patrol north of Go Dau Ha and asked them to stop at the MACV dock for assistance. Then he went down to the dock and used one of their sets.

"He claims to have intelligence that he feels he can rate Alfa-One that could have a great deal to do with your op tomorrow morning." Alfa-One was the best intelligence available. It meant that the source was totally reliable and you could bet on the information. The scale went all the way down to Foxtrot-Six meaning that neither the source nor the information was worth a shit.

"The word he has is that there's going to be two fairly important North Vietnamese cadre, together with at least a three-man security force, crossing the river tonight in the area of the Tan Trang. Coming from Cambodia and being alone, we can assume these guys are in some sort of specialized advisory capacity. They're probably en route to Saigon to join the pre-Tet buildup that's in progress there. The problem is that they will no doubt make at least a short stop wherever a small Viet Cong concentration is.

"Since the people who have the pilot and who will be making the deal with us comprise what amounts to the first VC force inside Vietnam along the route Mendez expects these people will take from Cambodia, the situation becomes sticky for us. Selling an American back to the Americans would be out of the question with a couple of cadre nosing around. The cadre would no doubt demand right then that they shoot the guy as an expediency. And that would be that."

Morelly nodded silently, not desiring to speak. He had just burned the roof of his mouth and the tip of his tongue with an accidentally large gulp. Franklin looked from him to Hagren and then to Sturgis. Then back to Morelly, who continued to nod.

"Burned my tongue." Morelly saw Hagren restrain a laugh. The two men looked at each other. Across ranks, a mutual respect allowed Hagren to be openly amused by a superior officer who had done some damage to himself.

"Well, we're all ready to get under way," Hagren said, trying to take Franklin's attention off Morelly and savoring the thought of an impending ambush at the same time.

"You want us to get under way and pick up Mendez?" Morelly asked, choking slightly as he caught his breath.

"No." Franklin shook his head. "I don't want that guy along until he has to be. Do you?"

"Hell no!" answered Morelly.

"I got all the pertinent information over the radio from him anyway. To the best of his knowledge, the crossing will likely come out of the small canal right south of the Tan Trang. I'd guess they'd cross directly to the opposite bank, paddle the sampan up the east bank to the mouth of the Tan Trang, then turn in and move up the canal. If I were you . . . come here," he gestured, turning toward the map. "I'd set up your boat right across from the mouth of the Tan Trang, on the west bank. You'll have a good view up the canal and downstream. Have Sturgis set up on the east bank, upstream, so he can watch upriver in case they cross to the north.

"Shall we just grease 'em?" Morelly knew the answer before he asked the question. The Vam Co Dong was a Free Fire Zone outside of the villages between 1900 at night and 0500 in the morning. A sampan on the river during those hours was fair game although some patrols tried to stop the sampan and take those embarked into custody. Morelly had never experienced such an attack of fair play. Technically, of course, the Rules of Engagement called for first firing warning shots and calling for the sampan to halt. In Vietnamese, naturally.

Morelly, and most of the Chiefs and other Patrol Officers in the division, believed in firing at least fifty warning shots, from all barrels on board, all on target. That way, one could always be certain that the sampan would stop.

"I'll leave that up to you," Franklin answered dryly. "Just remember that if you do pick them up, you'll have to drop them off at MACV in Go Dau Ha and fill out all those forms and answer a lot of questions and you'll be on a tight schedule anyhow."

Hagren laughed and turned around toward Sturgis, who smiled, "I doubt it."

"OK," Morelly said. "Then if we make contact with the sampan, we'll report the outcome and proceed to Go Dau Ha to pick up Mendez."

"Right. Then from then on, the rest is as we discussed it. So good luck. Seawolves are standing by at the YRBM if you need them. Get under way as soon as you can. Make your best speed up to the Tan Trang, and get your ambush set up as quickly as you can. For all we know, these guys may have already crossed but if they haven't, we don't want to give them any more time than we can help."

"Well, shit," Hagren said, pulling himself up from his chair and downing the last of his coffee. "We're ready."

NINE

A few minutes and some fumbling later, Morelly had found his pistol and gun belt amid the dark shelves of replacement parts in the Supply Shack and was making his way toward the boats.

The long-barreled Colt .38 was his pride and joy. No one that he knew in Vietnam had one except Shuster, who was now in pieces in the CONEX storage box. He had bought it at the Marine Recruit Depot PX in San Diego just before leaving the States. Being contraband in Vietnam, he had lied past the Air Force customs men when he had landed at Tan Son Nhut Airbase. The fact that he had done this made the weapon seem that much more valuable. He realized that he would probably never be able to get it back to the States, but he found himself hardly concerned with that at the moment. With the lightweight weapon now around his shrinking waist, Morelly felt more secure outside the camp than he had on his own cot amid the rats.

The fetid but cool air blowing up the canal felt refreshing as Morelly made his way through the tangle of barbed wire that separated the camp from the canal and the PBRs. As his eyes continued to adjust to the darkness, he looked up, searching for the moon. The sky was partially shrouded by clouds, but the moon shone through unchallenged, casting a silver gray light on the two green hulls moored side by side. Further down the canal lay the two additional boats recently arrived from the YRBM to stand by on Franklin's orders.

The moon would be up until dawn, which would be both good and bad. Having a little light was an advantage in that it definitely made it a lot easier to see where one was going. Morelly hated to have to spend an entire night watching the radar and trying to keep a Coxswain from running straight ahead when the river took a sharp left. On the other hand, the Viet Cong had the same moon. Since the Vam Co Dong was all hostile territory, the bright moon gave Charlie the upper hand. He could remain unseen in the shadow of the thick riverbank foliage no matter how bright the moon might be. A PBR, however, might as well be carrying a rotating beacon atop the radar dome. Every PBR sailor knew that the chances of his getting the first shot in any engagement on the river were virtually nonexistent. Being heard a mile away and seen driving up the river made ambushes a way of life for the PBRs. Fortunately, it was relatively easy to patch the fiberglass boats.

For the river sailor, the first or last quarter moon was the best time to be out. There was not enough light to be well seen, but at the same time there was just enough to effectively use the precious Starlight Scope. Large and heavy, the multi-thousand-dollar Starlights were kept under lock and key until legally signed out, for one patrol at a time only, to a responsible officer or petty officer. By absorbing moon and starlight and multiplying it several thousandfold, the observer could, in fact, see in the dark. With a ten magnifying power, he could see the enemy long before the enemy could see him. It greatly improved the odds what with the other fellow having nothing going for him but his good luck.

On pitch-black moonless nights, however, the advantage for either side was zero as long as everybody kept quiet. It became a nerve-wracking game. Commies trying to cross the river and PBRs quietly lying to, engines and radios dead, under a concealing clump of foliage. On a dark Vietnamese night, one could barely see who is standing a foot away. The winner in such contests is the side with the best listeners. If the Americans hear a Viet Cong moving in the dark, he's as good as dead. But if Charlie hears the Americans first, he'll either open up with his own ambush or, if he is in a non-combative mood, he will back off and go another route.

When it rains on the river, the situation becomes totally untenable. If anyone ever locked himself in a closet and turned out the light, he'd know how dark it got. It could not be any darker in the real world. Then add rain. The raindrops sound as though they weigh at least five pounds apiece as they hit the water. The night becomes a loud, steady hiss in the ears. Fortunately, the Viet Cong cannot see or hear either. There were recorded incidents of Viet Cong unknowingly paddling their sampan directly into the side of a hidden PBR. In such cases it became a question of who was quickest on the draw. One can imagine a poor gook trying to get rid of his paddle and find his AK-47 in a tipsy sampan. That is usually his last sampan ride.

The partial moon now setting could be trouble, Morelly thought, but chances were that if the prisoner pickup were to be made, it would be daylight, or nearly so, anyway. And the moon would be a help in detecting the expected sampan crossing.

The boats were impressive in the moonlight. In the slight breeze, the American flag floated lazily from the staff atop each canopy. As Morelly stepped onto the bow, he could see Hagren standing on the starboard gunwale, fresh coffee cup in hand.

"Got everything ready to go?"

"Right, sir. Got all the extra ammo on board. Had a little trouble getting the M-79 flares but we scrounged twenty off the Army. Fuckin' YRBM won't give you nothin' more than what they think you ought to have. Like they know what we need. They got their head up their ass sometimes."

"Well, I knew you could handle it with your powers of persuasion."

The big frame let out a laugh. "Yeah, I got it all. By the way, there's some hot coffee down in the engine compartment."

Morelly thanked Hagren and stepped down into the Coxswain's Flat. The Navy, he often thought, had suffered one of its rare attacks of common sense when it put together the River Patrol Boat. Thirty-two feet long and ten feet wide, it was as fast, maneuverable and well armed a boat as anyone could ask for under the circumstances. Its only drawback was no protection.

The forward deck contained nothing but a large metal ring into which were mounted a set of two fifty-caliber machine guns. As Morelly walked aft, McGinn had a red flashlight out and was working over these weapons—his babies. Firing white-hot incendiary rounds the size of a man's thumb, these were the PBR's heaviest armament. It was bad news when they jammed in a firefight. McGinn repeatedly cocked and dry-fired both weapons, making certain they were working perfectly.

The deck behind the superstructure was low inside the shell of the boat. On either side the gunwales came up to the average man's mid-thigh. While under way, it was here in the Coxswain's Flat that the Boat Captain and Patrol Officer spent most of their time. The Boat Captain had his steering wheel at waist level and his control console of Stewart-Warner gauges in front of him. By his right hand were four levers. One set, the throttles, controlled the rpm's of each of the two engines. The other two controlled the "gates" in the stern, and both could be manipulated with one hand. With the gates all the way up, the powerful streams from the water jets blew straight astern, pushing the boat ahead. Drop the gates down over the jet streams and that water was deflected 180 degrees, back under the hull, pushing the boat backward. Thus, even with the throttles wide open, the Coxswain could propel the boat from full ahead to full astern by yanking back on the levers that controlled the gates. In doing so, a PBR's bow would plow under water and the boat would go from twenty-five knots to full stop in little more than its own length.

Standing beside the Coxswain, the Patrol Officer controlled the Raytheon 1900/N Pathfinder radar and two radio microphones whose small speakers were mounted on a stanchion next to his head.

To the right of the flat, a small doorway led down to

a tiny sheltered area under the fore deck, affectionately called Chief's Quarters. The two AN/VRC-47 radios, one with Secure scrambler gear attached, took up the entire starboard bulkhead. Despite its cramped inconveniences, it was the only dry spot on a PBR during a tropical storm.

Aft of the Coxswain's Flat, the engine compartment housing the two GM diesels stretched all the way across from one side of the boat to the other and rose to the level of the gunwales. The hinged soundproof engine covers that swung up for repairs formed the deck upon which the midships gunner's M-60 light machine gun and M-79 Honeywell grenade launcher were mounted.

As Morelly stood waiting on the gunwale, the engine covers remained open as Raymond poked around in the dark depths of the large compartment. After two years and close to 300 combat patrols as an engineer, Raymond knew all there was to know about how to make a PBR run and run and run.

Unfortunately, the engines were not the only mechanical devices that were required to function flawlessly. To enable it to maneuver in shallow water, a PBR utilized two Jacuzzi water jet pumps, rather than protruding rudders and propellers, for propulsion. Located in the stern, on either side of the single deck-mounted fifty-caliber machine gun, the pumps drove the PBR by sucking water up through grates in the bottom of the hull and blowing it out the stern in a powerful jet stream. But the pumps were extremely delicate and easily fouled. Not only would they suck up water through the grates, but they also devoured grass, weeds, snakes, anything they could get their suction on. And when its pumps clogged, a PBR stopped dead. For the boat's low-ranking Seaman, cleaning the pumps was a never-ending ritual. Morelly watched momentarily as Lemon hunched over the starboard pump and lobbed hands full of grass over his head into the dark current.

Morelly threw his flak jacket over the doorway leading to Chief's Quarters and turned to pick a cup off the Igloo water cooler. In the engine compartment, Raymond finished his work, arched his already tired back, and started to climb out.

"Morning, Price. How about passing up the coffee before you get out. How are the engines?"

"Yessir," he answered cheerily. "These fuckers will run to the end of the world. Which, by the way, would probably be a fucking-a better place to be right now than here."

He replaced the pot between what would be some very warm engines and climbed out of the compartment, letting both port and starboard engine covers slam closed with a bang. He began wiping his hands with a filthy rag. "Go ahead and light 'em up, Hag."

Hagren punched both starters, one right after the other. The covers upon which Morelly had taken a stance began to vibrate as the throaty diesels came to life in the quiet night.

Raymond grinned as he stepped down into the Flat to look over Hagren's shoulder at how the gauges were reading. "They're sweet, boss," he said.

"OK, Hag," Morelly replied. "We're all good. Let's rock 'n' roll."

"Yessir. Price, bring down the flag and case it below. Bring in the anchor, Mac."

Raymond pulled the steel flagstaff out of its holder atop the canopy and began rolling up the flag. McGinn picked the anchor out of the wire on the bank, dropped it onto the fore deck and began taking in one of the two lines that bound PBR 716 to Sturgis's 714. "Lemon, cast off your line back aft there."

Although Navy regulations demanded that the colors be flown, especially when going into battle, common sense dictated a contrary policy. A great, colorful banner flying atop the superstructure certainly had its place, but such a game of nighttime hide-and-seek was not it.

Turning around, Morelly saw that Sturgis had already backed off the bank from his position along Hagren's starboard side and was now backing around Hagren's stern, up the canal away from the river. This maneuver would allow Hagren to back off the bank, turn about and move right out onto the river. Sturgis would then simply fall in astern.

It was a simple maneuver to be sure, but such coordination never ceased to impress Morelly. He was certain the two men had not given the action a thought, much less talked about it. It was simply a form of reflex. An instinctive action based on many days and nights together in these boats, watching each other, learning each other's reactions, helping each other. Just as Sturgis knew to back off and clear upstream, so Hagren knew that Sturgis was right then executing this maneuver. With only the slightest glance over his left shoulder, Hagren authoritatively gunned both engines astern and cut his wheel sharply. Once in the middle of the canal, he dropped his throttles to dead idle and lit a cigarette, his last of the long night. Raymond darted from one side of the engine covers to the other, shining his red flashlight overboard toward the waterline, checking for the overboard discharge which would indicate that the engines were drawing in cooling water properly.

"You got discharge starboard . . . got discharge port."

"Roger that, Price." Hagren called over his shoulder. Then to the crew: "Gentlemen, look sharp. We are ON the river." He pushed the throttles ahead, and eased his boat out of the canal onto the hot, dark and mean Vam Co Dong River.

TEN

Morelly looked back on the fading yellow lights of Tra Cu. A dump. A pit. It only looked good when they were going out on a patrol. Looking good was all relative.

He saw a couple of the Green Berets standing by the wire, watching the boats make their way out onto the river. Morelly gave a slight wave—a "see ya later, this is no big deal" kind of wave . . . low-key bravado. Bullshit was more like it. He got two similar nods in return.

"Grease a couple gooks for us, Navy," one of the soldiers called, flicking his cigarette butt into the water.

Morelly waved again in recognition. They for sure had no idea where the boat was headed. Maybe they cared, maybe they didn't. After all, the Greenies were all now John Waynes. As for the sailors, well, they were just the River Rats. The sailors. The swabbies. Whatever.

The river sailor had been a misunderstood individual since his creation four years earlier. He worked in desolate, remote areas on a demanding schedule that had him on patrol more often than he was off. His habit of wearing cut-off greens and T-shirts was construed as a lack of discipline. His bandying about of nicknames for officers and senior petty officers alike was disrespect.

In fact, his dependence upon his mates and his Patrol Officer was total and vice versa. For four or five men alone in a small boat, there was no place to hide. There was no alternative to performance. Experience had honed professionalism and individual skills to a fine edge and ragtag appearances and apparent disrespect were tolerated as a concession to the extraordinarily high caliber of the River Rat's performance and, of course, to the oppressive fucking heat.

"Lansing, this is Lansing Victor," Morelly said as he keyed the mike of his primary radio. "Under way at this time."

"Roger," Post's voice crackled above the engine noise. He should have been relieved by now, Morelly thought, unless he had decided to stay up and see it through the night. That would probably be the case.

"You put the radar on standby, Hag?"

"Yessir. Should be warm by now."

Morelly reached down to the left of the dark round screen and flicked the Off-Standby-On knob all the way to the right. As the eerie green image began to brighten behind the rotating sweep line, Morelly swung an opaque plastic shield across the set, thus limiting the emission of telltale light to one small rectangular opening in the center. Through it, he could see the contour of the river banks begin to take shape, running parallel to one another, equidistant from the center of the scope.

"I think it's on quarter-mile scan, sir."

Morelly nodded to himself, switching the scan knob over the two miles. The green disappeared, then quickly reappeared with the next sweep and the twisting river was outlined for a distance of two miles north and south. Morelly adjusted the intensity down slightly then flicked the set back on standby, satisfied that it would be tuned and ready if he needed it. The occasionally clouded moon would be bright enough for navigation although for the moment his delicate night vision, impaired by the radar, was not quite normal.

Both boats were now running at their 3,000-rpm top speed. Unloaded, a PBR at 3,000 rpm's would rise out of the water slightly and plane the surface with its flat bottom—getting "on step" the sailors called it. As it was, Morelly estimated they were making no more than twenty-two knots, which was less than reassuring. He reached up onto the shoulder-height superstructure and dragged his flak jacket into his arms. Slipping it on, he looked around the boat to see that the crew had theirs on. They did. Over the barrel of Lemon's fifty in the stern, Morelly watched the moonlit white water, glittering as it rose and fell splashing from the slicing bow of Sturgis's boat just astern.

Rounding one bend after another, Morelly recognized in the distance the dark shadows of the broken tree line that was Hiep Hoa. Hagren knew not to ask for instructions with regard to a speed change while passing through the village. Perhaps absentmindedly, perhaps to reassure Morelly that he knew what he was about, he pushed his throttles ahead with a bang of his palm on each lever. Nothing changed, for Hagren had known he was running flat out all the time. Sturgis, too, had unquestioningly maintained speed. In fact, it appeared that he was closing ever slightly.

Stepping outside the Flat, Morelly picked up one of the M-16s hung on the ceramic splinter shield outside Chief's Quarters and stepped up onto the engine covers. He laid the weapon athwartships on the canopy top and began to strain his eyes ahead in an effort to pick up any movement in the darkened village. The west bank was still level from the burning it had suffered after Franklin's firefight and Morelly imagined it would be only after the Americans removed themselves from the river that reconstruction would commence.

Candlelight could be seen flickering dimly inside the Catholic church but other than that, all was dark. Too dark, perhaps. But Morelly wondered only briefly about it, then dismissed the concern, having learned some time ago that attempting to outguess a Vietnamese was pure folly and could only be done through sheer luck. There were patterns of fear, however, which applied to all of human nature. Late in the afternoon on the day Franklin's patrol had been ambushed, Morelly had passed through the village at idle speed. Although he would be a hostile intruder twenty-four hours later, he had felt himself, at the time, required to make the usual friendly gestures. He had begun to wave along with Raymond who was beside him on the engine covers.

"Sir," Raymond had said, lowering his hand. "I don't see any kids."

Morelly had stopped waving and picked his binoculars off the canopy top. He could see no children either. The elders were not even taking notice of the passing boats. Any other time men, women, kids and dogs would have been down at the water's edge screaming and pointing their bony fingers into their gaping mouths. But this time they were impassive. Turning around, Morelly realized that the west bank was nearly deserted, with only a few women mingling around the wood and grass hootches. Although Morelly had radioed Tra Cu and informed them of these observations, such evidence was obviously not merit enough to begin running patrols full-bore through the village. That night, of course, Franklin's forward gunner was killed by rocket fire and the Navy's attitude toward Hiep Hoa changed.

But now there was only the candlelight in the church and Morelly felt he could only take that for what it was worth: another fray in his harried nervous system. The sugar mill also was dark and menacing, but that was not unusual. No one ventured near that structure either by day or by night since everything that could be unbolted, unscrewed or ripped up had been stripped from its abandoned guts by the grateful townsfolk.

"Come down to 2,000," Morelly said to Hagren ten minutes later, as they approached the Tan Trang Canal. The engines immediately died to a low rumble and the stern rose gently as the wake backwash rolled under the transom and slewed the bow slightly sideways. Morelly had not felt it necessary to radio the maneuver to Sturgis and, as he expected, even in the dark Sturgis had only closed a few yards before observing and executing the lead boat's speed change.

"Price," Morelly said, turning to Raymond before ducking into the Flat to be beside Hagren, "keep an eye on Sturgis so we know where he is when we set up."

"Right, sir."

"O.K. Hag, come down to idle and let's hug the left bank." Morelly spoke quietly as though it would make a difference with the twin diesels announcing their presence.

"Here, Hag," Morelly said as the boat eased to a point almost directly across the river from the mouth of the Tan Trang.

Hagren abruptly spun his wheel to the left and pulled the left throttle towards his body. All forward motion stopped and the boat swung as though on an axis as the astern thrust of the port engine bit into the black water. McGinn scrambled out of his forward mount and crouched on the bow, holding a nylon line in his right hand and warding off low foliage as the bow eased into the bank. Seconds later he secured the boat with a slip knot tied to a tree limb. Had the current been any stronger, the knot would not have held. Fortunately the tide was slack, having not yet begun to flood. Testing his work, McGinn yanked the knot free, then quickly retied it. Both engines choked and died and the world fell quiet except for the drone of Sturgis's engines as PBR 714 maneuvered into the opposite bank less than a hundred yards upstream. As that noise faded and died, all was silent.

Morelly glanced at his watch. Five after one. It had only been forty-five minutes since Post had awakened him and this now-unchangeable risk called an operation had been put into motion.

"Puttin' the radios all the way down," Hagren whispered. Morelly nodded and stepped out of the Flat, up onto the engine covers. Hagren would remain at the wheel, ready to light off the engines and get under way in an instant. McGinn continued to sit on the forward gunwale, cradling an M-16 and peering intently into the underbrush. It was one of the three vulnerable areas for the still boat. Should a large force come upon the boat undetected, the ensuing firefight would be wholly on the enemy's terms and casualties on the boat would surely be high. On the Vam Co Tay River several weeks earlier, a VC had crawled up to within a few feet of a boat one night and lobbed a grenade aboard. After some seconds of frantic scrambling in the dark, the man on the bow found the grenade and threw it overboard. A boat on the My Tho River in the lower Mekong Delta had not been so lucky, and the seaman who dived on the grenade in the stern had become the Force's second Medal of Honor winner, posthumously.

The second area of vulnerability was directly across the river. There an enemy force, easily out of earshot of the boat, could set up a major ambush at its leisure, then open fire on the immobile boat. One hit in the stern would sink the boat or at least destroy the pumps and kill any means of propulsion.

The third vulnerable area was directly under the boat. The commies were known to have sappers, as they called their frogmen, who, as previous members of the South Vietnamese Navy, had received the best underwater demolition training in the world at the Naval Amphibious Base in Coronado, California. Raymond had received the Bronze Star earlier in the year when he had detected a sapper under the hull of his boat and dived into the water, K-bar knife in hand. Following a brief struggle, he had brought the swimmer to the surface alongside the boat. As his mates reached overboard and grabbed his shirt to keep him afloat, Raymond slit the man's throat and let the corpse slide quietly beneath the surface. He had then proceeded to inspect the boat's hull, discovering that the sapper had not had time to plant an explosive.

"Bring me some M-16 clips," Morelly whispered to Lemon as the latter brushed by and quietly disappeared into Chief's Quarters. He reappeared seconds later with a fifty-caliber ammo can full of M-16 clips in one hand and an M-79 grenade launcher in the other. Two bandoliers of grenade rounds were slung across his chest.

"I got H.E. and illumination rounds, sir," he said, setting the can of clips on top of the canopy and scrambling quietly back to his post down in the stern.

Raymond remained immobile beside his M-60, its belt of linked ammunition trailing down to the large rectangular metal box at his feet, filled to overflowing with fresh, unrusted rounds. He stood erect, scanning the river to the north with the Starlight Scope.

"Sturgis is just north of that big tree stickin' out up there," he said to Morelly, turning and handing him the scope. As Morelly focused on the foliage in the area Raymond had designated, Raymond picked up the binoculars from the canopy top and continued to scan.

In the dense undergrowth, Morelly could barely make out the silhouette of 714's stern as it protruded into midstream. The Vam Co Dong was no more than fifty yards wide at that point. Sturgis, on the opposite bank and slightly to the north, was invisible to the naked eye. What the brush did not conceal, the moon-cast shadows of the trees on the water did. Morelly could not tell for certain, but he imagined his boat was about as well covered as Sturgis and felt that such protection was satisfactory.

ELEVEN

Minutes passed slowly as Morelly and Raymond continued to watch the river to the south, swapping Starlight and binoculars frequently as the intense green light of the Starlight became unbearable to the eye after five or ten minutes of strain. Morelly pulled his wristwatch down from under his shirtsleeve where he had moved it to cover its luminous dial. The light from a watch could be seen up to fifty yards away. As he glanced down it seemed to shine like a hundred-watt bulb. The time was 0145. Morelly's back began to ache and his legs yearned for a seat. His eyes burned and itched, their measure being gradually taken by the eerie Starlight. Although the night had cooled to probably the high sixties, sweat continued to drain from his pores.

"Sampan!" Raymond whispered excitedly, pointing with one hand as he held the heavy Starlight in the other.

"Lemme see." Morelly reached for the scope. "How many do you make it?"

"Five. Maybe six. They're at midstream now. Here."

Morelly focused a mere twenty to twenty-five yards away from the boat. There, five men sat one behind the other in a small sampan. The sampan was no more than twenty feet long and under the weight of five men, even little ones, the wooden craft was nearly under water. The bow and stern pointed from the water, but Morelly imagined there could be no more than a couple inches of freeboard at the sides. The man in the bow and the one in the stern were both paddling. The three in the middle were apparently sitting as Morelly had seen Vietnamese do so often in an effort to keep the center of gravity as low as possible. Even so, he thought, they must be getting wet with every slight tip of the sampan. The man directly behind the bow oarsman was cradling a weapon, while the two behind him simply seemed to be holding on.

"Warning shots?" Raymond asked urgently, pulling his M-60 from its cradle on the splinter shield and resting the butt on his right hip. The ammunition belt clinked metallically and through the Starlight, Morelly saw the man in the middle look up. Even in the hazy green glow, the sampan was close enough for Morelly to see clearly the wide-eyed fear and disbelief on the man's face as he must have known what was about to happen. Morelly and he could have spoken to one another they were so close. The armed man raised his weapon in readiness as the oarsmen stroked faster.

"No warning. Hit 'em now. OPEN FIRE!" Morelly yelled the last command aloud, wanting to be sure everyone immediately understood him since the sampan now neared the east bank and safety. "Lemon, stay off the fifty. It'll break up the sampan. Get a flare in the air."

He dropped the Starlight on the canopy and picked up the M-16. He had never checked to see that a round was in the chamber. He did not have to because he knew McGinn would have put one there when they had gotten underway. He flicked the selector from Safe past Single to Automatic and raised the weapon to his shoulder.

Before he could complete this motion, he heard the "thunk" from Lemon's grenade launcher and caught the white sparkling trail of the flare as it ached skyward. Simultaneously, Raymond opened fire with his M-60. Had the enemy soldiers then jumped overboard, they perhaps would have had some shadow of a chance at survival since Raymond's first rounds were low. The red tracers struck the water and ricocheted over the sampan into the trees beyond. As the flare burst overhead, bathing the entire scene in a pure white light, Raymond walked the rounds to the sampan and locked on. The man in the stern was blown away outright. Every sixth round out of Raymond's rapidly firing weapon was a red tracer and Morelly saw at least three red streaks flash from the machine gun and disappear into the man's body. His paddle flew into the air and the barrage lifted him from the sampan and knocked him backward over the starboard side.

In that same split second, Morelly was squeezing his trigger, firing with both eyes open, not aiming but rather just sighting down the barrel. His fire caught the fourth man back from the bow at the same instant that Raymond's swinging machine gun zeroed in on him after eliminating the first soldier. Red tracers from two angles formed a cone from the PBR to the man's body. In a flurry, his shoulder and head disintegrated and he disappeared over the side, tipping the sampan and dumping the three remaining men into the river. The sampan righted itself and drifted peacefully. Lemon put another flare in the air as the first began to die.

"Underway, Hag. Let's go. There's three of 'em in the water."

Hagren lit off the engines and began to back out of the foliage. McGinn had already released the knot and slipped down into his gun tub. But rather than converge on the action, as was certainly his fond wish, he kept his twin fifties trained on the west bank, ready for an ambush by a possible security force. The radios crackled to life as Hagren somehow found a second to turn them up.

"Keep it on 'em, Price," Morelly shouted above the steady staccato hammering of the M-60. "Don't let 'em get their heads up." Throwing his expended first magazine onto the canopy, he found another and jammed it home. He wanted Sturgis to recon the west side of the river by fire but did not want to take the time to get on the radio and try to be heard over the noise. Looking back and seeing the white wake of Sturgis's boat as it moved in fast to assist, Morelly turned and sprayed the contents of his magazine along the west bank. In the two seconds it took to empty a twenty-round M-16 magazine, Sturgis's boat had taken its cue and was pounding the bank with everything from the fifties on down.

Meanwhile, Hagren maneuvered rapidly downstream, jockeying his throttles to make the boat move ahead while keeping as much of the port side facing the target as possible so that all weapons could be brought to bear. Relieved of covering the west bank by the heavy fire of 714, McGinn swiveled his mount to the port bow, trying to find a target. A head bobbed up between the sampan and the PBR's bow, but neither Morelly nor Raymond had a shot until they could get to the port gunwale and take aim around the Coxswain's Flat.

"Port bow, Mac, in the water!" Hagren yelled. McGinn made a slight adjustment to his right and heaved the rear of the mount upward as far as it would go, depressing the barrels just over the gunwale. He clenched the electric firing handle and the weapon hammered. Bambambambambam. The head, waving both arms frantically in a desire to be saved, disappeared in tracers and frothing waters.

For a moment, all was quiet as both boats ceased firing. Morelly reloaded again while ordering Lemon to put another flare in the air. As the added light broke and bathed the river, both Morelly and Raymond saw movement on the edge of the river's east bank. Morelly had caught it out of the corner of his eye and it took him a fraction of a second to pinpoint the movement and get on target. Within twenty yards, a survivor attempted to claw his way onto the bank with his right arm. His left hung limply at his side. Raymond opened fire just before Morelly and the impacting rounds slammed the soldier into the mud. In his excitement, Morelly emptied his magazine before he realized that Raymond had done the job and then some. The man's back and head dissolved amid spatterings of mud, water and leaves.

The river fell quiet again. PBR 714 prowled the west bank in silence as Hagren cautiously maneuvered close to the drifting sampan. Lemon now had two flares in the air simultaneously and the area was as bright as the light of day, though its reach stopped at the dark edge where river met foliage. The sampan bobbed listlessly in the settling water. Hagren passed by one side at a distance of fifteen yards, idled downstream, then turned and approached from the other side.

"There's one around here someplace that we didn't get," Raymond said quietly, straining his eyes across the water's surface. "I'll put a couple of concussion grenades around the sampan and along the beach."

He replaced the M-60 in its swivel and ducked down to the deck beside the Coxswain's Flat. He picked four tall, cylindrical grenades out of the small arms locker and returned to the engine covers, handing two to Morelly, who threw one to the near side of the sampan and the other across to its far side. Raymond threw both of his between the sampan and the river bank. In rapid succession all four explosives detonated with a muffled "thummp whoosh" that spewed geysers of water into the air. The impact of a concussion grenade underwater could kill a man at relatively close range, crushing his body in its shock and throwing it to the surface. Morelly had heard of men who came "clawing their way out of the water," victims of such as experience. Actually, they would most likely be dead or at least be unconscious and dying when they were blasted to the surface. They would then sink below the water, perhaps to be found and added to the body count three or four days later when they rose, bloated, to the surface.

For a few brief seconds following the four explosions, the crew waited and watched. No one had crawled out of the water on the geysers. The last man may have been killed or he may have made it to the bank.

The "thunk" of Lemon's grenade launcher broke the

silence. Morelly's eyes focused automatically on the only foreign and attracting object then in his field of vision: the sampan. In the time it took the slow-moving grenade round to reach its target, nearly a second, Morelly had registered the scene vividly in his mind. Holding desperately onto the bow of the sampan with one hand, the bobbing head held its other hand aloft and waved, crying "Chieu hoi . . ." in a vain effort at surrender.

Lemon had had an illumination round—a flare—chambered in his grenade launcher and had fired it. There was no loud explosion. The projectile rammed perfectly into the middle of the contorted face which disintegrated in a hail of flying white sparks but remained afloat momentarily, pushed back against the sampan bow. The flare burned brightly in the cavity that had been a head. The entire crew watched in silent amazement as the sparkling light sank out of sight.

"Goddamn it," said Morelly, shaking his head. "I've never seen anything like that. Man, I've never even HEARD of anything like that. And what a shot! Man, Lemon, how long you been here in-country, son?"

"Roger that," Raymond said calmly, M-60 again at the ready but with nowhere to shoot. "That was beautiful, Lemon. An illumination round between the fucking-a-eyes. Sheeee-it."

With Sturgis covering, Morelly had Hagren move alongside the sampan. McGinn and Raymond lay down on the forward deck and, reaching into the sampan while Morelly shone a battle lantern over the side, the two sailors quickly retrieved four AK-47 Chinese assault rifles. All were loaded and all had their safeties off. But no one had gotten off a shot. Morelly tried to imagine how those men had felt in the seconds or split seconds before they died. He realized that he could not possibly think that deeply at the moment.

Satisfied that the sampan was empty, Morelly dropped a concussion grenade inside it as he called for Hagren to move out at full speed. As the PBR pulled away, the sampan splintered into flying bits and disappeared.

The last dying flare, swaying beneath its small nylon parachute, faded from white to pale yellow to a glow of orange and was gone. Hagren adjusted both throttles to 2,000 rpm's, turning his wheel to achieve a wide lazy circle. As his boat's head swung to north, he quickened his speed. Sturgis drove across Hagren's wake and fell in directly astern. Save for a few bits of wood that would be lost in the night's current, the river became its dark and quiet self once again.

"Make max speed for Go Dau Ha," Morelly said, stepping into the Flat and picking up the Secure radio mike.

TWELVE

Within an hour, both boats began slowing as they approached the town of Go Dau Ha. Morelly had called in the preliminary report on the successful ambush, which Franklin had received with strangely little elation. Lights still glowed in Go Dau Ha and from midstream, Morelly could see several South Vietnamese sentries walking their beat. The fish market, the center of seemingly all life and activity during the day, was now totally deserted. It was a concrete structure resembling a Roman forum to some degree, with pillars around it on three sides. It had been built, by the French no doubt, right at the water's edge, permitting easy access for either buyers or sellers arriving by sampan. Morelly could make out the shadowy figures of two soldiers, cigarettes glowing, lounging just beyond the market's naked electric lights.

The Army dock where Morelly was to meet Mendez was fifty yards upstream from the market. Built of no more than ten empty fifty-five-gallon oil drums lashed together by God knows what and covered by a thin sheet of corrugated metal, it had originally been constructed by the Army for the use of their small armada of dark green Boston Whalers. For a PBR, getting alongside was something like the Queen Elizabeth easing itself into a tugboat slip. At any rate, the dock was now in tatters, victim of some hard knocks and the strain of holding the relatively large PBRs against the strong current. Rather than perhaps being the straw that broke the camel's back, Morelly opted in favor of the marketplace itself. Besides, he favored the market because the crew could get off the boats and relax in the relatively secure area.

The two Vietnamese soldiers stepped out to the edge of the market as Hagren maneuvered PBR 716 in to tie up. McGinn leaped from the bow, Lemon from the stern, both with line in hand, and each took a few turns on the nearest pillar. With a slight cough the engines died to idle, then fell silent as Hagren pulled the air cutoff valves shut.

"*Chau, Ohm*. Hello, gentlemen," Hagren waved cheerily, stepping out of the Flat and up onto the engine covers. The soldiers, M-16s slung over one shoulder, waved back, grinning, and began babbling rapidly to each other. When two or more Vietnamese were talking, Morelly had observed often, nobody listened. Everyone talked as fast as he could, apparently disregarding the fact that everyone else was also talking. These two, standing side by side, both talked furiously, pointing at the weapons, the radar dome, the antennae, each paying no attention to the other as he pointed out what seemed to interest him most.

"We got time to cook?" Sturgis called out, pulling

his boat alongside Hagren's and cutting the engines as his crew secured the two boats together. Morelly looked at his watch. It was slightly after three and Mendez was not expected until four. Morelly wondered if Mendez had received word that the cadre had been wiped out.

"Yeah," Morelly answered. "Hag, why don't you have Price get the stove and whip up a stew?"

"Yessir." But he did not need to turn and relay the request to Raymond, who was already heading for Chief's Quarters to get the stove.

"I'm a-goin'," Raymond yucked, always in the mood for his own homemade stew.

"Cut your radios, Sturgis," Morelly said, stepping back into the Flat. "You'll have to keep them on the rest of the morning after we leave, so there's no point in killing your batteries."

Morelly picked up the Secure microphone, keyed it and waited a second for the "beep" that told him the set was functioning and his message would go out scrambled. Anyone monitoring frequency 55.05 with a regular radio would hear only squeaking static as the transmission was made. If there was no beep, one could always be certain that his message was either going out in plain language or was not going out at all. Now, there was no beep.

"Lemon, check the Secure set down in Chief's Quarters, will you. See if the green light's on."

"Right, sir." Lemon promptly disappeared below. "Orange light's on, sir. Must have been hot." He flicked the toggle switch to the up position. "Green light now." The set having overheated and cut off, Morelly reminded himself to shut it down and give it a rest after he completed his call.

Beep. "Lansing, this is Lansing Victor, over."

Some minutes later, Morelly had relayed a complete Spot Report to Franklin, including the exact coordinates of the engagement, time of commencement and completion of the action and total ammunition expenditures of both boats. Although he had not recovered the actual corpses, Morelly was certain that all five men had died. When he came to the last line of the report calling for a classification of enemy casualties as either "killed in action, probable" or "killed in action, body count," he unhesitatingly claimed all five as the latter. A good body count always did wonders for the division's morale, for they felt that they were then giving Charlie some of his own medicine, especially in an ambush situation such as this one.

For the Navy, a body count was generally very hard to get. After a firefight with an enemy ambush element along the shore, the boat crews could not leave their boats and go ashore looking for bodies. By the time Army troops were moved to the scene for a sweep, the living VC were gone, having dragged the dead with them. The only time a good body count could be obtained was during daylight when a helicopter was immediately overhead to make the count. But a chopper, especially an Army chopper, as often as not fired a few rounds and claimed the kills as his own. A ground sweep could uncover a few bodies if the number of casualties had exceeded the number of survivors but, in general, the sailors had to be content with trails of blood leading into the brush away from the scene.

Raymond had lit the small tin fuel-burning stove and was heating fresh coffee by the time Morelly finished his report and stepped from the gunwale onto the concrete market floor. "Gonna make us some strong coffee too, sir," Raymond grinned as he knelt down over the little camp stove. Morelly could hear water already boiling as Raymond continued to dip a small coffee-filled flare parachute into the water, being careful not to let go of any of the chute's nylon strings lest the grounds slip into the pot.

Most of both boat crews and the two Vietnamese sentries were now gathered around McGinn and Hagren as they carefully examined the captured arms under the market's brightest bulb. Hagren, McGinn and Lemon were telling stories of the turkey shoot as quickly as they could get them out of their mouth. It was obvious that Lemon would be the hero from the start, having recorded his first kill with an M-79 flare. Popping a zip in the face with a grenade round showed some "real class" as one of Sturgis' crewmen put it. That kind of talk gave some indication, thought Morelly, of the depths of insanity to which they had all slipped. War was like that. Enough insanity to go around, but at a controlled level so that it somehow seemed entirely reasonable.

The Vietnamese, obviously impressed by the weapons and beginning to understand how they had been acquired, grunted and grinned.

"These VC guns, you know," Hagren tried to explain. "We *soc mau* VC down the river." "*Soc mau*" seemed to mean not just that they had killed the VC, but that they had killed the shit out of them. A state of desirable overkill, like winning a football game 78 to nothing.

"Oh, ya? Soc mau VC? Ya, ya."

"Ya, *soc mau* five VC. How you say 'five' in Vietnamese, Mr. Morelly."

"I forget. Try 'cinq'."

Hagren held up five fingers. "*Soc mau* five VC. You *biet*? You understand? *Beaucoup* VC."

"Ya," one soldier said as they both nodded. "I biet. Ya, beaucoup VC."

"Funny motherfuckers," Lemon muttered as Hagren allowed each one to handle one of the rifles.

"Ah, numbah one," they both agreed, pointing to a rifle, then to themselves. 'Numbah one' was the top rating on the Vietnamese ten-point scale for virtually everything.

"Fuck no you can't have one, you motherfuckers." Lemon seized both weapons back with a scowl. The sentries recoiled, smiles frozen.

Hagren snorted. "Lemon, back off. Leave 'em alone. They're just a coupla slopes tryin' to have a good time."

It was quickly decided that Lemon should have one of the rifles and so, certainly, should Raymond, who had caught the crossing with the Starlight. The other two, Hagren stated, should naturally go to the Patrol Officer and the Boat Captain, himself. Morelly agreed but quickly declined, requesting instead that his trophy be given to McGinn who had gotten one kill for sure and who, Morelly could see, was a bit hurt at being the only 716 crewman not to rate a weapon.

"Don't be too surprised," Morelly added to the group, "if some or all of these guns get called in to Saigon or Binh Thuy."

"Goddamn brass," Lemon wailed with great authority. "Sittin' on their ass. They want a war trophy, why don't they fuckin' come out here and get one?"

"And why don't you fuckin' shut up, cherry boy," laughed Hagren. "Help McGinn clean the weapons while Raymond's doin' chow."

"I don't know why, Lemon," Morelly said, glancing away from the light in an effort to keep the crew from interpreting his smile as an endorsement of Lemon's disrespectful obscenities.

"You gents want to get some cups," Raymond called. "This coffee ain't gonna keep hot all night." Several men stepped back onto their boats for cups, Hagren returning with two, giving one to Morelly. Morelly became first in line, an honor that he did not care for but knew not to decline.

Minutes later Raymond had mixed and heated a pot of various C-ration meats spiced with A-1 sauce and began serving up his concoction. Morelly found it delicious, considering the raw material available, and finished with a satisfying burp and an urgent need to crap. Since no facilities were readily available, he took a roll of toilet paper from the boat and made his way to the stone steps descending to the water from the side of the market. At the water's edge he turned and, after carefully and thoroughly scanning the area with his flashlight to assure himself of the absence of rats, dropped his trousers around his ankles. Squatting low, he hung his butt barely out over the water beyond the lowest step.

Many of the men, he included, had found that the easiest way to complete this particular exercise was to stand on a PBR gunwale and hold onto the canopy stanchion, much like an ocean sailboat racer heaving out to windward in a strong blow. It got the butt well out over the water and, with a clear vertical drop, there was little danger of making a mess unless the wind was particularly strong and unfavorable. A short directive from the Force headquarters, however, had recently ordered this practice abandoned. Evidently, a sailor on the Mekong

River had placed himself in such a posture and unfortunately lost his grip on the stanchion. Perhaps being a weak swimmer to begin with, he no doubt found it doubly tedious to remain afloat since he must have had great difficulty using his legs, they being bound around his ankles by his trousers. One shipmate dived overboard in a rescue attempt, but to no avail. The body was recovered thirty-six hours later, washed up to the river's edge some twenty klicks downstream.

When Franklin had shown him the casualty report on the incident, Morelly felt somewhat ashamed of himself when he totally cracked up over Franklin's reference to the possible content of the letter that the man's division commander must have written to the bereaved parents or wife.

"What the fuck could you possibly say?" Franklin asked, tears welling up in his eyes. "'He died doing his duty?' 'If only he had learned to swim with his pants down?' 'The wrong dump at the wrong time'?"

It was hardly a funny incident, the loss of life in such a pointless fashion (assuming that life can be lost in a fashion other than pointless). Had the circumstances been somehow different, Morelly would have been rightly appalled by it. But he laughed. He laughed at a sophomoric and not-even-funny joke. Why? Why indeed. But sometimes any pressure release, no matter how slight, was nonetheless a release.

For five solid minutes, Morelly and Franklin had laughed nonstop. Tears had rolled down their cheeks and they had gasped to catch their breath. These were desperate men.

Now, whenever he crapped in a situation such as this, he thought of that poor bastard, being swept downstream drowning. Did he try and pull his trousers up? Or did he just try to keep afloat and . . . Morelly smiled and shook his head, as he did each time he recalled the incident.

THIRTEEN

At precisely 0400—four o'clock in the morning—the hooded headlights of a jeep bounced towards the river through the hootch-lined roads of Go Dau Ha's residential area. With an unoiled screech, the jeep came to a halt at the head of the Army pier. For a second the engine idled roughly, then revved and lurched the vehicle ahead as the driver inadvertently popped the clutch. The jeep recranked and moved toward the market. Morelly walked to the market's edge to meet the fat little man.

"I thought you would be back there at the Army pier," Mendez said as the driver brought the jeep to another abrupt halt, jostling Mendez nearly out of his seat.

"Right."

"But you weren't," Mendez persisted, still sitting, glaring slightly.

"Right. Too crowded."

Mendez peered quizzically upstream to the vacant

Army pier. But realizing the futility of the conversation, he sighed and heaved himself out of the jeep. Without a word, the driver had popped the clutch once more and was off with a lurch and a whine of the tough little engine. The bottom line was that the Duty Driver is never happy when he has to make a run at four in the morning.

"Mr. Franklin relayed to me that the cadre we were concerned about were taken care of."

"Yes, that's right."

"You're certain that you accounted for all of them?"

"I saw 'em all go."

Mendez nodded. "Good. Did anyone appear to have a radio?"

"Nope."

"Anyone else around? Any security forces on the beach?"

"Not that we saw. It's a Free Fire, you know. We put in H&I fire on both banks. We got nothing in return. More than that, we don't know for sure. If I had to guess, I'd say they were alone and we got 'em all. Clean."

"Excellent." In Morelly's mind, Mendez was EXACTLY the kind of little spook, as they called all the in-country spies, who would mutter something like "excellent' in that situation. He was doing, like, a bad Peter Lorre.

Most of both boat crews were still lounging in the market area as Mendez walked past them without a word and boarded the boat nearest the wall.

"Let's saddle up," Morelly said to Hagren's crew as he stepped aboard, past Mendez and onto the outboard boat. Following the meal, Hagren and Sturgis had gotten their boats under way and changed position. Thus

Hagren would be able to get away easily and quickly, without Sturgis having to man and move his boat again. "We'll be taking this boat, Mr. Mendez."

"Yes, of course. Ah . . . does your crew here understand what we are doing?"

"I believe so. The Boat Captain has briefed them on what we feel they should know. This is a good crew. They're young, but they're professionals. They know what they're doing."

"Fine. Then I suppose we should be going. When we arrive at the sugar mill at Hiep Hoa, it must be five o'clock exactly. We may be a minute or so early or late, but no more."

"0500. On the nose. No problem. Light 'em off, Hag. Let's go."

"Aye, aye." A River Rat never would say "aye, aye" unless he was trying to impress a stranger or was being sarcastic with a superior whom he little respected. Morelly knew the latter was not the case.

"Additionally," Mendez said, raising one hand as an afterthought, "there can be no smoking after we begin to approach the point of pickup. I am to signal the man waiting for us with my lighter. We would not want him to be confused by lights that we had not discussed or agreed upon."

"These men never smoke on this river after dark," Morelly lied only slightly. "As long as you are on board, I would ask you to follow that same precaution until daybreak."

"Very well," Mendez nodded, a bit chagrined.

Morelly stepped down into the Flat beside Hagren and flicked the radar scope on. Satisfied with the clarity of its green sweeping picture, he switched it back to standby.

Mendez had seated himself at Raymond's feet on the engine covers. Apparently in a thoughtful daze, he removed a pack of cigarettes from his pocket and began to light one.

Raymond bent down over the man's shoulder. "Sir, uh . . ."

"Sorry," Mendez said, turning his shiny, greasy face up toward Raymond.

Obviously bored with the boat ride, he passed the remainder of the trip in silence, watching the water go by. His faded green camouflage fatigues blended perfectly with the rushing water and thick foliage. At times, a quick glance by Morelly caught only what appeared to be a brown head floating near the gunwale.

The wind was cooling but Morelly continued to sweat as he had been doing since picking up Mendez. The silent little man represented the reality of the whole thing. He gave Morelly the creeps. The mission gave Morelly the creeps—for all kinds of reasons. But, on balance, Morelly was a good officer, a good man, and he would see it through if there was any chance at all to bring out one of their own, an American.

As the PBR sped down the river, Morelly made his way up the starboard gunwale, holding onto the canopy frame tightly. When on a combat patrol, Morelly experienced grave pangs of nakedness and fear whenever he did this. For the three seconds or so that it took to walk from the engine covers to the bow, a man was helpless, hanging on to a narrow bit of the boat's edge in the dark. He dreaded the possibilities of an ambush during those few seconds.

Stepping onto the bow, he sat down on the foredeck
and leaned against the superstructure next to McGinn,
who was out of his mount and sitting on the port gunwale. The rushing wind was pleasant and the dark foliage
on both sides sped by. As was often the case, McGinn
looked scroungy, even in the moonlight. Having a baby
face, his periodic attempts at a moustache or beard continued to prove fruitless and left him looking simply
unkempt. His uniform helped his appearance little—
faded fatigues with sleeves ripped off and trousers cut off
just above the knees. He wore a camouflage bandana
around his neck.

He cradled an M-16 in his lap. His technique in the
event of an ambush was to put the weapon on full automatic and empty the magazine in the few seconds it took
him to leap into his mount.

He probably never hit much with that first burst,
but that really mattered little. When Charlie begins seeing muzzle flashes coming back at him, he tends to put
his head down, stick his rifle over or around or through
whatever he's hiding behind, and blindly pull the trigger.
Thus, Charlie doesn't hit much either.

"We supposed to pick up some gook here, right sir?"

"Right."

"You expect we'll get to pick up a POW?"

"I don't know. Looks like it. If Mendez can make
the deal with the VC we're about to pick up."

"I'd love to do that. Something like that would make
a lot of this bullshit worthwhile." He smiled. "Anyway, I
bet we'd get our names in the *Stars and Stripes*. 'Specially
if it was for picking up some Army dude. He a pilot or a
grunt?"

"Pilot."

"Shit, I don't know why they picked a PBR, that's for sure. And going with only one boat. I mean, I don't mind going and all. I just wonder why they picked a PBR to do it."

"The best of a bunch of bad options, Mac."

"Gotcha, sir."

Realizing that Hiep Hoa was rapidly approaching, Morelly called back into the flat for Hagren to slow to just above idle, giving the boat a speed of eight to ten knots, depending on the current.

He walked back aft to the engine covers where Mendez was now standing and leaning against the canopy, chin resting on folded arms.

"Price, go down below and get a flak jacket for Mr. Mendez."

"That's OK. I never wear the things."

Technically, Morelly should have insisted, but he let the subject drop and Raymond moved back to his machine gun.

It was 0458 as the boat eased up to a point just north of the sugar mill. Morelly stood beside Mendez on the engine covers and both men strained, Morelly with Starlight Scope, Mendez with binoculars, to see anyone moving in the area where they expected the contact. There were several people walking about, but one could distinguish only shapes.

"Keep watching," Mendez said, taking his eyes from the glasses and reaching into his pocket. He pulled out a Zippo, struck it twice and slipped it back into his pocket.

Dim yellow light from awakening hootches in the background made observation difficult. Morelly switched to the more powerful binoculars but they tended to put all objects in the field of view in the same dimensional plane. Thus in the darkness where relative size and fore-ground and background terrain could not be used to pin-point distance, it became difficult to be certain whether lights were right on the bank or quite a few yards back.

The shapes moved slowly before Morelly's scanning glasses. Some were obviously women with large baskets atop their heads. Others presented the small hunched silhouette of the very old. A few dogs had begun to bark. Then a spark and a flicker. Another spark and a small flame. Unmistakably close to the bank. Then it was quickly out and the yellow lights from behind shone through again.

A shadowy figure, partially concealed by low scrubby foliage, squatted on the river bank in front of the still-closed market. Morelly could not be certain if this figure had been the one to strike the lighter, but he was the only one visible in the immediate area. Morelly strained harder, boring in on the figure with his tiring eyes. Focusing totally on one subject as he was, Morelly began to be able to make out a head and arms. The head turned from side to side, looking up and down the dirt roadway that ran alongside the river bank. As quickly as the figure flicked his lighted cigarette into the water, he fished into this shirt pocket, drew out a fresh one and struck his lighter again.

"That's him," Mendez said calmly.

"Go in slow, Hag." Morelly poked his head down into the Flat and pointed over Hagren's shoulder. "He's squatting in front of that market."

Morelly picked up two extra magazines and an M-16 and again made his way up the gunwale to the fore deck. Mendez followed, unarmed as far as Morelly could see.

McGinn had moved into his tub as he felt Hagren alter course and begin heading straight for the river bank.

"Stay in the tub, Mac," Morelly said. "Keep your guns on full cock, keep them aimed ahead and slightly elevated. No matter what happens, don't fire unless I tell you to, OK?

"Yessir."

Hagren idled down just before the boat hit the bank, but there was still a light bump as the bow struck the wet mud. He then set the throttles ahead to keep the boat beached. Morelly sat on the starboard gunwale trying to take in everything that was happening on the shore. The Viet Cong, dressed in a white shirt and shorts, had begun to drift away from the open area toward the shadows of a closed store. He made no signals and for a moment Morelly tensed severely as he felt the fear begin to tie up his guts—like butterflies but with some major attitude. The patrol had been drawn, alone, into the beach. And they now sat dead in the water with only the forward fifties and his M-16 bearing on the bank. As the man in the white shirt continued to drift further away, Morelly's mind began to race. He prayed that the man had not been a decoy into an ambush. He literally prayed. God, don't let that son-of-a-bitch have been a fucking decoy. Don't let this be a trap. "There are no atheists in foxholes," the old saying goes. Or anywhere else in Vietnam.

Mendez quickly moved in front of McGinn's machine guns and hopped gingerly off the bow. Morelly moved around to cover him as he walked toward his contact. McGinn swiveled his mount to port to cover the flank. To Morelly, the possibilities for disaster seemed endless.

But within sixty seconds Mendez was back and he and the typically lean-looking Vietnamese climbed aboard.

Morelly followed them aft down the gunwale. Mendez gently pushed the man down off the engine covers toward Chief's Quarters.

"Just cruise up and down off the town here while I talk with him down below."

Morelly nodded as Mendez and the Vietnamese slipped into the dark doorway. Mendez turned on a large battle lantern next to the radios and Morelly let the waterproof plastic door cover roll down over the entrance to keep the light from escaping.

Hagren quickly backed off the bank, manipulated the throttles to turn the boat in its tracks, and gunned it out toward open water. Within minutes the boat was cruising up and down in front of the sugar mill.

FOURTEEN

By 0600 the sky had begun to brighten and PBR 716 had made no fewer than ten laps up and down the same piece of the Vam Co Dong River. With the first clearly discernible light of dawn, Morelly had permitted himself a cigarette and now stood on the engine covers, studying the clouding sky. Rain was nearly unheard of at this time of year, but the sky looked ominous.

Since Mendez and the Vietnamese had adjourned to Chief's Quarters, Morelly had heard nothing but sporadic jabberings. Interestingly, the conversation was all in Vietnamese. Evidently the VC had at least not said he wouldn't deal. One could be fairly certain of that. Wrapped in his own private thoughts of what the coming day could conceivably bring, Morelly did not hear Mendez step out of Chief's Quarters and up onto the engine covers beside him.

"This man and I have made an arrangement," he said

slowly to Morelly who started and turned at the sound
of the voice. Mendez made an indication to the now
meekly smiling, nodding Vietnamese standing at his elbow. For an instant Morelly felt himself revolted by the
thought of dealing with this little Viet Cong and then
allowing him to walk blithely off of a boat that was under his command. His greatest urge in that instant was
to draw his .38 and empty it.

"Uh huh, and now I suppose the gentleman wants
to be dropped off somewhere in particular?"

"Yes, that's right." Mendez reached around, grabbed
the tiny man by the left bicep and hoisted him up onto
the engine covers. They spoke a few words of Vietnamese at one another. The VC nodded furiously and pointed
to a small tree line on the west bank north of the sugar
mill. "He wishes to be let off up ahead there, on the left
bank."

"Not a problem, gentlemen. Hag, make for that tree
line on your left."

"Right, sir."

"He has the money?" Morelly asked, glancing down
at the rectangular brick wrapped in newspaper and string
that the little man clutched tightly in both hands. He
looked like he was gripping a chicken to keep it from
getting away.

"Yes, he has." Mendez appeared to take a deep breath
and sigh heavily, as though he knew he had crossed the
Rubicon and now all that remained was for him to find
out what fate would be his. With a few more words in
Vietnamese, both Mendez and the stooge made their way
to the bow.

Within minutes Hagren had maneuvered into the
thick of the tree line, directed by urgent hand signals

from the VC on the bow. At the instant of contact with the bank, the man gripped his precious package even more tightly in both hands, darted off the boat into the under-brush and was gone. He had no doubt considered his release somewhat of a minor moment of truth, for he could not have been certain that the Americans would allow him to take such a great deal of money and walk off with it, having only his good word to rely on in re-turn.

Hagren quickly pulled back off the bank and slid out into midstream. "Price, come here and take it for a minute," he called back over his shoulder. Raymond scur-ried down into the Flat and Hagren emerged onto the engine covers, standing beside Mendez and Morelly. "Well, what's the story?"

"We shall go from here to the Tan Trang Canal, as we suspected we would have to do," Mendez said. "Are you familiar with the canal?" Both men nodded. "It runs to the east from the river for about five kilometers up to the town of Tan Trang. The pickup will be made about four kilometers up the canal. When we see two tracers fired from south to north across the canal in front of the boat, we are then to proceed another one hundred meters and beach the boat on the south bank. The prisoner will be there in the foliage, perhaps some distance back from the canal bank.

"There could conceivably be local loyal Viet Cong sympathizers in the immediate area, so our man's captors do not wish to lead the pilot directly to our boat and help him aboard. They would fear being seen and re-ported as having executed an obviously traitorous act. Also, they no doubt feel they would stand a reasonably good chance of being shot by us for their efforts.

"Consequently, what they will do is allow the man to escape, so to speak, and follow him toward the position of our boat, firing over his head. At the same time, you will have your forward machine gunner fire bursts into the air, thus aiding the pilot to fix our position and make his way to us.

"I have received assurances sent from the VC who hold our man that there are no hardcore NVA troops in the immediate area of the canal. However, these men have been in hiding, and out of circulation, for several days, so we cannot depend one hundred percent on their information being up-to-date. I'm sure you understand that. So, if you are ready," Mendez wound up with a sigh and a fat little flourish of one hand, "I think we should begin right away."

"Yeah," Hagren noted, "before it gets hotter than a bitch."

"Or rains," Morelly added.

Hagren shrugged, not finding the prospect at all funny. "This could turn into a real mess if we're being set up."

"I don't think we have too much choice at this point, Hag. If we back out now, who knows what happens to the pilot? They may figure he's just not worth anything to us—or to them—and kill him."

"If they haven't already," Hagren shrugged again, taking a long drag on his cigarette and flicking it over the side.

"Plus," Morelly added with a grin, "we aren't fucking pussies. We may be on a pretty stupid operation here but, Boats, we aren't pussies."

"Roger that, sir. OK. Let's rock 'n' roll."

"Let's go over the firing and all with the crew first."

Hagren nodded and moved into the Flat, taking the wheel from Raymond. Morelly could see that he had begun giving instructions to Raymond, so he moved forward to speak with McGinn. As usual, McGinn was sitting on the gunwale and he nodded several times, not saying anything, as he received his orders.

"No matter what goes on," Morelly finished, "don't fire directly into the trees unless I tell you to. We don't want to go all the way up the canal and then shoot our own man just when we're about to pick him up. OK?"

"Right, sir. Sir, do you think this is really for real and that the VC wasn't just handing us a bunch of shit to get the money?"

"It could be, Mac. But I don't think so. If we get hit on the way up, we'll try and turn around and come out. There's no point giving up two or three of us for one POW. That's bad arithmetic."

McGinn grinned and nodded. "Roger that. Especially if the two was you and me, right, sir?"

"Right. But we're gonna get this guy. We're gonna save this guy, this pilot. If he's up there, no way he's not coming out with us."

"We're for that, sir. We're ready to go."

Morelly moved back aft and saw that Raymond and Lemon were now in the stern, beside Lemon's machine gun, talking.

"Lemon," Morelly interrupted. "Price telling you about what we're doing here?"

"Yessir," Raymond said. "I jes' told him and he don't seem to get what I'm trying to say here. I mean, he thinks it's outta sight." Raymond laughed. He slapped little Lemon on the shoulder with a smile. "You dumb motherfucker. I hope that gun of your works 'cause you're gonna need it, no shit. You, my friend, are about to be in your first firefight and you can jes' hope it ain't your last."

"Well, maybe he's right, Raymond," said Morelly. "Maybe we're gonna get up that canal, grease a bunch of NVA and come back out, on step, with the pilot."

Raymond shook his head, grinned through his shiny black face and hopped up onto the engine covers. Morelly squatted down to talk face-to-face with Lemon as Raymond passed behind him, removed the ammunition belt from his M-60 and began checking the breach and action.

"Lemon, it's almost for sure that we'll have some contact here. I would say that the best thing for you to do is not to think too much about it now, if you can, and just make sure everything back here is working. Especially that fifty. You ought to get an M-16 back here with a few magazines or a few more H.E. grenade rounds for your M-79 just in case this fifty does jam up on you. Now you understand about firing?"

"Right, sir. I fire in the air over everybody's head."

"No. We're not going to do that with you. I'm having Mac put a few bursts into the air since he's up front and we'll be going into the beach bow first. What I want you to do is to cover our ass. We'll be beaching on the south bank, so I want you to cover the north bank with your fifty. If you see any movement, let it go. But if we start taking fire from the tree line, you cut loose and I mean don't fire in the air. Just do what you can to suppress fire until we can start getting off the beach. Price will be able to swing around and back you up with the M-60 unless we start getting it from both banks. Then I just let him fire wherever we're getting it the worst."

"That means, then, that I got the north side all alone if Price starts firing someplace else?"

"Right. But they're afraid of that big fifty. Those white phosphorous tracers are something to see coming at you. Just remember to pick your target and fire bursts to save your ammunition. Fire at people or muzzle flashes, not at the trees. OK?"

Lemon shrugged his shoulders and stooped to pick up his flak jacket. "OK, sir. You're the boss. I'll take care of things back here as much as I can."

Morelly stepped back into the Coxswain's Flat, keyed the Secure mike and called Franklin.

Beep. "Lansing Victor, this is Lansing," came the reply, loud and clear.

Beep. "Roger, ah, we have the thing set to go off here in a few minutes. It's up the Tan Trang Canal like we thought. We're en route there now. Have you got anything as far as weather down there?"

Beep. "That's a negative at this time. I'll get in touch with Atlantic Island just to make sure the Seawolves are still up. I'll be back to you in a minute," Franklin said, signing off with his final "out." Morelly replaced the mike and looked again at the sky. To the north and east it was clear. Broken clouds drifted across Cambodia to the west. But the sky to the south was becoming blacker by the minute. And under that dark cover, Morelly imagined the Seawolf helicopter gunships sitting wet and closed on the YRBM-14 as sheets of water whipped across the flight deck.

Beep. "Lansing Victor, this is Lansing." Franklin's voice was tired and drawn. "I relay from Atlantic Island, weather there is beaucoup rain. Heavy squalls, ceiling under one hundred feet. Visibility is sucking big time."

Beep. "Roger, copy. Then what's our status?"

Beep. "As long as the weather is just a pocket around their area, the birds will lift off for a scramble and try to fly out of it. Word is that they expect it to blow over shortly. Atlantic Island Actual claims he went back to Illusion One and got a go-ahead on your ball game. Repeat, you have a go-ahead direct from Illusion One."

Beep. "Yeah, roger that." Not wishing to take final responsibility for allowing a single patrol boat into hostile territory with possibly no air cover, Getzel had radioed the River Patrol Force headquarters in Binh Thuy and tried to put the decision in the hands of the Commodore, Captain McGinnis. The Commodore no doubt cagily reaffirmed his "confidence" in Franklin's "decision" while at the same time noting that if the mission were aborted at this point, someone would have to account for why the little Viet Cong was allowed to skip off with 200,000 piasters. Mendez would carry no blame since it would not be his decision to call it off.

Probably the Commodore's foremost fear would be that after getting into this operation, the Navy would duck out with what the Army would suggest was insufficient reason. Then the Army, in a one-upmanship effort, would send a force into the area and attempt to find the pilot and bring him out over land. The Army could conceivably be successful, making the Navy look very bad. Worst of all, the Commodore would look like a pussy in the eyes of Admiral White in Can Tho and perhaps even in the view of Admiral Zumwalt in Saigon. But if the operation proceeded and even if it was unsuccessful and the Force had to scratch off a few men and perhaps a boat, the Army would still owe the Navy some valuable respect if nothing else. Morelly's mother would receive a medal to remember him by and would not the entire thing have been worthwhile? Trying to be as honest with himself as possible, Morelly was not altogether certain that it wouldn't.

Beep. Franklin was back on the air again. "I think we'll be able to get you air from someplace if the Seawolves are rained out. Army air at Can Tho or even Tay Ninh City. Wherever it has to come from, I'll get it for you if and when you need it."

For Morelly, that assurance was enough. If Franklin said he would get air cover, then he would get air cover even if he had to fly it himself.

Beep. "Roger. Thanks, Emmitt."

"This is going to be some day, Mr. Morelly, sir," Hagren said as Morelly replaced the microphone on its hood above the radar scope.

"Yeah, I bet you're right about that. Where are we now?"

"Just passed Hotel One."

Morelly knew exactly where checkpoint Hotel One was, but he turned to the map mounted on the splinter shield at his side anyway and rechecked the distance. It would be less than two kilometers to the mouth of the canal. Looking around, he satisfied himself that everything was as ready as it could be.

McGinn, standing on the bow, had just pulled the green nylon groin protector from down in the gun tub and was wrapping it around his waist. Made of the same material as the flak jacket, the groin protector zipped up the front and snapped under the crotch, giving the wearer the appearance of being dressed in a pair of oversized green jockey shorts. Few of the men wore it as a rule, but most of them kept one on board in the event of having the good luck to be warned that imminent contact was definite.

Raymond had donned one himself and he was now in the process of pulling a heavy bulletproof vest over his head, on top of his flak jacket. Morelly had only seen him wear the vest once before, that being another canal incursion when the vest fortunately proved unnecessary. Standing amidships on top of the engine covers, Raymond was the most exposed man on the boat. He had a shield up to his thighs, but nothing else besides his vest. Now, however, he became the only man on board who could take a round in the chest and live to talk about it.

In the stern, Lemon stood tensely behind his weapon, aiming it over the port gunwale in the direction that would become north when the boat entered the canal. Mendez remained on the engine covers, leaning against the canopy. No doubt, Morelly thought, he understood that authority had changed hands and he could no longer direct the actions of these men. They were doing their own jobs, doing what they had been trained to do. Mendez became a passenger with no control. It was clearly a role in which he seldom found himself.

FIFTEEN

Rounding a bend in the river, Morelly saw the Tan Trang Canal ahead on his left. Hagren pulled the wheel slightly to the right and began hugging the bank as he prepared to make the wide, swinging left turn into the canal. Seconds later, Morelly felt the hull roll to port under his feet as the boat leaned into the turn. White water flew by the gunwales and the rooster tail from the stern spouted high in the air. It was a perfect, beautiful insertion as Hagren drove diagonally across the river and hit the canal entrance dead center, midway between each bank.

"Shallow," Hagren called over the whine of the engines. His head turned to catch a glimpse of the wake. The rooster tail was nearly flat now, hardly visible over the transom. In deep water, it shoots high in the air. In shallows, there is less room for turbulence to be created beneath the surface and thus less of an opposite reaction into the air. Morelly felt the boat rise almost imperceptibly and get on step as the water blasting astern from the Jacuzzi pumps now concentrated all its energy on pushing the boat ahead instead of dissipating itself in the form of deep water turbulence. As long as it did not get too shallow, Morelly thought, the boat would be a hard target to hit.

Moving slightly northeast on the canal, PBR 716 was fortunate in not having to challenge the morning sun head on. Instead, the rising orange ball glinted only occasionally through the dense foliage that lined the river bank to their right.

The boat was running well, Morelly thought, and chances were they would be back out in a matter of fifteen minutes, twenty at the most. The boat skimmed past a burned-out pagoda on the north bank and Morelly swung around in the Coxswain's Flat to see if he could find it plotted on the map. In general, pagodas and other religious structures were excellent landmarks because they were often the only thing still in the same place ten or twenty years after the making of the map. Whole towns and villages could change their physical location, but a pagoda or its remains would stand indefinitely. Even their ruins must be sacred, Morelly had guessed, for a destroyed pagoda was never, to his somewhat limited knowledge, razed to the ground and rebuilt. Rather, it was left exactly as the invaders, whomever they had been in that particular decade, had left it.

He was not surprised to find this pagoda plotted. From it he realized that they had already transited halfway to their objective although it had seemed like only seconds since they had left the Vam Co Dong. He picked up an M-16, stepped onto the engine covers and laid it across the canopy top. His left elbow rested on the empty flagstaff holder. For a moment he wanted to break out the colors and unfurl them, bright and free. The pure white knights charging headlong into battle, their banners flying, their shields flashing in the sunlight. Yeah, go tell that to your daddy. Plus, it would flap in Raymond's face.

Somewhere slightly ahead of the boat and to the north, there were the cracks of automatic weapons. Morelly's mind dropped its idyllic dreams and locked onto the present. He realized the shots were close, perhaps very close, and he sensed Raymond moving quickly behind him, jumping from the port to the starboard side of the engine covers, swiveling his M-60 180 degrees to the north bank. Simultaneously, Morelly had his M-16 rifle off the canopy and was swinging to bring it to bear on the north side of the canal. Mendez jumped from the deck up onto the engine covers directly in front of Morelly, his helmeted head striking Morelly's weapon and knocking it into the air.

"Watch yourself, big guy. We got some fire up ahead," Morelly shouted, urgently but without alarm, as he firmly pushed the heavier man back off the engine covers and into the Coxswain's Flat. Morelly could pinpoint no muzzle flashes and had seen no tracers in the air, but as he quickly scanned the canal bank he saw a thin layer of gray smoke hanging in the tree line just forward of the boat's beam. He aimed, clicked onto automatic and emptied half his magazine into the thicket. In that one second Raymond, standing at Morelly's side, was on target, firing short, penetrating bursts. With the sound of rapid explosions, Lemon opened fire with his big fifty caliber. His first rounds struck the water halfway between the boat and the bank, but he quickly walked his tracers up onto the bank and the entire tree line seemed to shake from the bullets.

As Lemon had commenced firing, Morelly saw several muzzle flashes in the trees and the green tracers began zipping toward them. These light automatic weapons were no contest, however, as both Lemon and Raymond locked onto the flashes with long bursts of fire.

McGinn had realized that the after gunners had the situation well in hand and swiveled his mount to cover the south. Mendez, however, returned to the engine covers, this time behind Morelly's shoulder. The PBR sped past what had appeared to be simply an opportunistic ambush by some Viet Cong who happened to be near the river when they heard the boat coming. The boat sped out of range, and both Lemon and Raymond ceased firing. There was no longer return fire from the tree line, only the rapidly dissipating gray smoke.

"Thunk," the grenade launcher echoed in Morelly's ear. Turning quickly he saw Mendez, weapon in hand, anxiously watching the flight of his just-launched grenade. Morelly looked back in time to catch the round's detonation on the bank, a good twenty yards short of the target area.

The flying clumps of mud fell like large raindrops on the water and amidst the trees. "I'm a bit out of practice with the M-79." Mendez smiled sheepishly and stepped down off the engine covers to the main deck, cocking the launcher open and throwing the spent casing overboard.

"Everybody good?" Morelly called, loud enough to be heard by everyone on board. All hands answered in some version of the affirmative. "Everything OK, Hag?"

"Right sir," Hagren answered after a moment's pause to examine his gauges and dials. "Wait one," he added after keying first the primary, then the secondary microphone. "We got no beep on the Secure."

"Aw, shit." Morelly pushed past Mendez and moved down below into Chief's Quarters. Even in the daylight that streamed through the doorway, the small area was very dark. Morelly saw immediately that neither the green "on" light nor the orange "off" light was lit. He reached up to a cubbyhole on the bulkhead, retrieved a battle lantern and turned it on the radios. The Secure set was dead for the duration with a single round through the scrambler key. Morelly glanced around to the port bulkhead and saw the small point of light that was the bullet's entrance through the hull.

Working quickly, he disconnected the Secure cable, replaced the protective cap over the outlet and flicked a toggle switch on the AN/VRC-46 radio from Secure to Clear. The radio came to life with its constant quiet static hum. He returned to the flat, keyed the secondary mike and heard the echo of its static in the loudspeaker beside his head.

"Hag, call Lansing and tell him we had contact and have lost Secure capability. We'll stay up regular secondary radio frequency." Morelly stepped out of the Flat. "This is not a good start, Mendez," he said. This first omission of the "Mister" was intentional.

"You have no casualties. What did you lose? Your Secure set, which you can do without anyway. You already have the coded message that is to be sent when the pickup is made. That can go out in the clear."

Morelly could feel the blood rushing to his head and his eyes began to water. "And what happens on the way out, for Christ's sake? We aren't like the Goddamn Army. We can't sneak around and find another way out. We gotta get out the same way we came in and those zips, if there's any left, know that. Goddamn!" He turned and snatched the primary mike from Hagren's hand. "What's Franklin say?"

"Nothin' sir. Just rogered."

Mendez moved off to the side, again a bit chagrined. Indeed, he had not thought ahead to the details of an exit strategy, the reality of which was that they were going to have to come out the same way they went in. Not good, it somehow dawned on him for the first time.

"Lansing Victor, this is Lansing." Franklin was coming back on the radio.

Morelly keyed his mike to answer. "Roger, Lansing, this is Victor."

"Victor, abort the mission. I say again, abort the mission."

"Lansing, this is Victor. Understand mission abort. Is that correct?"

"Roger that, Victor."

"Understood, Lansing. Mission is aborted. Out"

Before Morelly could cradle his microphone, an urgent voice squeaked over the secondary radio speaker.

"Lansing and Lansing Victor, this is Atlantic Island." It was Getzel. He was nearly hysterical. "I monitored the last from Lansing to Lansing Victor. This is Atlantic Island Actual. Lansing, I strongly suggest you reconsider mission abort. I repeat, strongly urge you reconsider your last, Lansing. How do you copy?"

"Roger, Atlantic Island, I copy. Break. Victor, you copy the last from Atlantic Island Actual?"

"That's affirmative." Morelly answered. "I copied his last. Understand negative mission abort is the order. Is that affirmative?"

"This is Lansing. Roger that is affirmative."

"Lansing, this is Atlantic Island. How do you read?"

"Roger, Atlantic Island, I read you loud and clear."

"This is Atlantic Island. Be advised that my last to you was NOT an order. Your Patrol Officer is on the scene." Getzel's voice had calmed down now to a placating high whine. "You two know what the situation is. I understand the ransom money has already been turned over, is that affirmative?"

Morelly stamped his feet on the deck in a gesture that he would normally never allow himself. "Listen to that! Hagren, listen to that sonofabitch Getzel!"

Hagren showed no emotion. "Yessir. I hear the little prick. But he's the boss, sir."

After a pregnant pause, Morelly heard Franklin come back on. "Atlantic Island, this is Lansing. That's affirmative. The agent with Victor has turned the ransom over."

"Roger. And does Victor's guest wish to abort the mission at this point?"

"This is Lansing. Wait one. Break. Victor, did you copy that last?"

"This is Victor. I copied." Morelly turned around and stared at Mendez. The big man shrugged and showed only the slightest hint of a smile. "That's a negative. He does not desire an abort."

"Victor, this is Lansing. How close are you to your target area?"

"It should be coming up shortly. Zero five minutes maybe."

"Roger, OK, stick with it for another few minutes. You copy?"

"Roger, that's affirmative. I copy. Out." Morelly replaced the mike on its hook. Only once before had he been on a boat so far to the north and still been able to pick up Getzel on the radio, from all the way down on the Vam Co River. And this had to be one of those days when the signal traveled unusually far. "Getzel, I'd like to get your ass out here one time," Morelly breathed through his teeth.

He felt suddenly very tired. Fed up. Nothing was rational. But that was nothing altogether new. Unfortunately, this time irrationality could cost him a great deal. Still, the orders—even though they were delivered in a cover-your-ass kind of way, were clear. Stay the course, get the grunt and shoot your way out—do whatever you have to to make it work.

"Mr. Morelly!" Hagren struck Morelly a substantial blow on the left bicep. "Up ahead."

Morelly glanced up to see two green tracers die out in their skyward arc from south to north. McGinn, down in his gun tub, was waving his arms urgently and pointing to a thick tree line along the south bank. "Where from?" Morelly asked, picking up a set of binoculars from a cubby beneath the radar.

"In the tree line. See those two tall skinny trees, the dead ones, side by side? Just past there."

"Right," Mendez agreed. "Just past there in the tree line."

"OK, one hundred yards past that and we'll hit the bank." Morelly heard himself speaking in a relatively nonchalant voice. He stepped out of the Flat, retrieved five M-16 magazines from the small can at Mendez' feet and stepped up onto the engine covers. He rammed one magazine into his weapon and forced the others into his cargo pockets. Holding his rifle at the ready, he set it on full automatic.

SIXTEEN

"You feel like I feel?" Raymond asked, standing beside Morelly, holding tightly to the pistol grip of his M-60. Morelly nodded his head in a gesture that was more emphatically affirmative than any other reply he could have made. Sweat streamed down his face, his neck. A tiny droplet hung on his right eyelid and was blown away by the rushing wind. He turned to Raymond who was blinking nervously. Their eyes met for a second. "Jesus loves you, Mr. Morelly." He was being sincere.

"And you, Price, I'm sure."

Mendez stepped onto the engine covers, grenade launcher in hand. "We're coming up on a hundred yards."

"I know." Morelly was about to order Hagren into the bank but now it would look like he was doing it solely at Mendez' suggestion. He hated the idea. "OK, Hag, hit it here."

The Downed Pilot Drill was taught religiously at

the Inshore Operations Training Center, but Hagren was about to become probably the first Boat Captain to use it in Vietnam as far as Morelly knew. It was a pretty cool move in inshore seamanship. The objective was to allow the boat to hit a hostile river bank straight in, the most desirable angle, without having to decrease speed in advance and maneuver unnecessarily if under fire.

The south bank being on the starboard side, Hagren swung the wheel hard to port as he jerked the port engine from full ahead to full astern. Morelly lurched forward against the canopy as the bow dipped and the deck beneath his feet quickly fell off to his left. The boat's forward motion stopped almost immediately and the craft began to violently churn its way through a tight counter-clockwise circle. A green panorama whirled before Morelly's eyes and he turned in the opposite direction to try and keep his vision fixed on the south bank. Hagren spun the wheel to starboard to prevent oversteer and thrust the throttles into neutral. The bow settled precisely as it should have. It had swung around 270 degrees, to point squarely at the south bank of the canal. But to push ahead at that point would be to make the drill's fatal error, for the frail boat would be caught in the strong first swells of wake water from the maneuver. Out of the Coxswain's control, it would have surfed ashore, ending up either high and dry on the beach or sunk with a crushed bow. But Hagren remembered his lessons and held the boat head-on to the bank as the swells rolled pleasantly underneath. When they passed, he gunned his engines ahead as if to smash the beach. At the last second, he backed down hard with both engines and the boat bumped to a halt, its bow dug a mere few inches into the mud.

In executing the maneuver, Morelly had had little opportunity to choose the best place to land since the point of impact was determined by the shape of the turn, which had commenced before the boat actually drew abreast of the site. As it was, they could not have picked a better spot. They had landed at a break in the tree line, evidently cleared some time before for the construction of a small hootch and pagoda, which were set back about thirty yards from the canal bank. The hootch, built of straw and bamboo, stood to the left of the clearing, while the remains of a stone pagoda lay to the right.

The clearing ran in a semicircle just behind the two structures, and extended for approximately forty yards along the water's edge. The pagoda was a little more than a pile of colored rubble, mostly a charred black or the original light blue. One wall of the pagoda still stood. The hootch, on the other hand, was immaculate. Originally, both pagoda and hootch had probably been destroyed together, but the latter had since been rebuilt. In fact, over the years, probably many hootches had been built and destroyed on that same spot.

As the boat came to rest, both Morelly and Mendez made their way to the bow and crouched on either side of McGinn's gun mount. There was silence except for the rumble of the engines. For what seemed like forever, every ear on the boat strained to hear and every eye strained to see. Something. Anything. For to find nothing could be the most ominous foreboding of all. Still, there was no sound. Morelly stood on the fore deck and turned around, toward Mendez.

"Pretty spooky. Those tracers, now nothing. You got any ideas, Mendez?"

"Mr. Morelly . . ." McGinn was standing erect in his

mount, pointing toward the hootch. "Outside the hootch. On the ground."

"Binoculars, Hag," Morelly called into the flat, afraid of what he thought he saw but knowing that it could not be ignored. He focused on the hootch, no more than thirty yards from the boat. Settled in the shaggy grass there could be no mistaking a part of a green fatigue uniform. The hootch doorway was open, but even through the glasses all Morelly could see were dark shadows with nothing discernible inside.

"We're gonna go check the hootch, Hag." Morelly picked up his M-16 and moved toward the bow. "Raymond, bring your sixty up to the canopy and cover up and down this side of the canal. Mac, cover us on either side of the hootch."

"You got it, sir."

"Come on, Mendez."

"Right behind you."

Both men stepped onto the bank and began to make their way toward the hootch, moving first to the protection of the pagoda wall. How many times Morelly had been told not to go ashore under any circumstances, he could not remember. "Your training is in riverine operations," the lecture went. "You are not equipped to go ashore and you have not been trained to go ashore. DO NOT EVER DO IT." But everyone did. Morelly himself had gone ashore on the Vam Co Dong several times to investigate the river bank for possible arms caches. His first such debarkation had resulted in the discovery of two fifty-five-gallon drums filled with Communist rockets, small arms ammunition and C-4 explosives. He had been congratulated for the discovery, as had the other

Patrol Officers who had found similar caches. But it often became a very volatile political situation.

When a Patrol Officer from 551 had gone ashore
with two of his men and they had been ambushed and
suffered the loss of one of the sailors, that Patrol Officer
had been removed from his job and sent to staff duty in
Saigon for the duration of his tour. On the other hand,
Lieutenant Hower with River Division 533 had gone
ashore with some men while patrolling the lower Bassac
River in the Delta. In an ambush, Hower died and was
posthumously awarded the Bronze Star. It seemed that
if one either accomplished his mission or died, he was
rewarded. If he encountered serious trouble yet still managed to escape alive, then his problems were only beginning. These thoughts knocked around in Morelly's head
as he debarked but, typically, they registered and were
gone before he had taken his first few steps.

Both he and Mendez reached the pagoda wall together, sliding into it slightly out of breath. "You know
anything about hootch searching?" Morelly asked.

Mendez nodded. "Some. I'll go first, you cover me
from here. As soon as I reach the hootch, you come on.
I'll cover you. I'll make for the left of the doorway, you
make for the right."

Morelly nodded. "OK. Go."

Mendez moved to the edge of the pagoda wall, took
one quick look around the side and was off. Morelly
stood to a crouching position and leveled his rifle over
the top of the wall. Mendez was running zigzag, low to
the ground, just like in the Army movies, except that
Mendez was a fat little guy. Morelly made a mental note
to be sure to do the same thing. Mendez reached the side
of the hootch and Morelly quickly followed. Both men

looked around them to the trees, thick and concealing of anything or anyone who was hidden in them. Mendez held up one hand, motioning for Morelly to remain where he was, and began to move toward the doorway.

It was one of the crudest booby traps in the world, but it still would have caught Mendez badly were it not for his surprising agility. He stepped into the doorway, placing the weight of his right foot on the flat plank buried beneath the dirt and grass. The plank sprung up, releasing the pin, which it held depressed. Swinging on hinges that secured it to the top of the doorway, a straw mat thick with deadly sharp bamboo punji stakes dropped forward. Standing directly in its path, Mendez had little choice as to what action to take. To jump forward would only be to run headlong into the stakes. And there was no room in the narrow doorway to move either left or right. With the grace and agility of a major leaguer ducking a beanball, Mendez kicked his legs forward and fell backward. Still, the lower stakes caught him as they swung through their arc, running a huge gash up his left arm and tearing away a small portion of his left ear. He screamed loudly for an instant, then rolled silently out from beneath the punji mat that swung above his head.

"Cut the mat down," Mendez said, crawling to the side of the doorway and propping himself against the hootch. "He's inside, staked out on the ground in the far corner. He's alive. Tied and taped. Watch for booby traps on the body. Fucking trap. Fucking gooks."

"No shit, Sherlock. We gotta get him outta here in a big Goddamn hurry." Morelly jumped to his feet, pulled his K-bar knife from its sheath and slashed the mat's straw binding.

"Motherfuckers," he could hear Mendez wheeze over and over through his teeth as the blood that continued to stream down his face and arm began to soak the grass.

Morelly rushed into the hootch and flattened himself against the grass wall, pausing momentarily as his eyes adjusted to the darkness. For a second he could hear nothing, then he caught a guttural grunt coming from somewhere inside the hootch. As he became able to make out shapes, he saw something moving on the ground a few yards away. Staked out spread eagle on the ground, the American was gagged with what appeared to be his own green T-shirt and was clad only in a pair of tattered fatigue trousers. His feet were bare and cut.

"Shit. That trap! I'm sorry," the pilot gasped as Morelly pulled the gag down around his neck.

"It's OK. He'll be all right. Just got his arm and the side of his head. You OK? Can you walk?"

"How far?"

"Just a few yards."

"Shit, yes. But my bet is we're all in deep shit now."

"They gonna try to whack us on the way out of here?"

"I don't know. I bet so. They set that trap after they had staked me here, so I didn't see anything else. Little fuckers are out there somewhere for sure."

"VC or NVA?"

"Both."

Morelly rolled his eyes to the heavens. "Great. Just fucking great."

The two men exited the hootch and Morelly turned to pull Mendez to his feet. As the three began running for the boat, the trees on the outer perimeter of the clearing immediately lit up with automatic weapons fire.

Mendez went down as a round burst his right thigh open and knocked him off his feet.

"Behind the wall," Morelly screamed to the pilot, pushing him in the butt toward the cover of the pagoda then sliding to the ground himself at Mendez' side. Morelly and Mendez were both still lying out in the open but, fortunately, it seemed like most of the enemy fire seemed to be coming from an area that was now partially blocked from the line of sight by the hootch. Still, tracers zipped from the woods on all sides and Morelly was aware of bits of dirt and grass being spewed into the air by near misses. He rolled over onto his belly facing the trees, raised his M-16 to his shoulder and emptied the magazine in quick short bursts. As he rolled onto his side to pull a second magazine from his cargo pocket, he became aware of McGinn's white tracers arching overhead. His best chance was to let the boat draw the fire while he tried to pull Mendez to the pagoda wall.

"Can you move?" he yelled into the man's good ear.

"Help me," Mendez answered with a violent shake of his head.

Morelly seized his collar and began to pull as Mendez scratched desperately at the grass with his good leg in an effort to help propel himself along. The fire from the trees had subsided only slightly although most of it was now being directed against the PBR. As red tracers began to fly from the boat along with the white, Morelly realized that Raymond had gotten his M-60 onto the canopy top and was into the action.

Morelly reached the pagoda wall and with a great effort yanked the heavy body around the corner to momentary safety. His hands were shaking and the knuckles of his left hand were bleeding, rubbed raw by the grass and dirt over which he had just dragged Mendez.

The braided lanyard, from his sister, was gone. It had been ripped off his wrist.

"Fuck, I'm sorry you guys got sucked into this," the pilot breathed.

"We're here to take you out of here, my friend, and that's what we're gonna do," Morelly said, drawing the Colt .38 from his hip and handing it to the man. "I think we'll be all right in a minute," he added as he watched Hagren maneuvering to swing the boat broadside to the beach. Raymond had stopped firing the M-60 and was hurriedly working over the Honeywell automatic grenade launcher. As the boat came about, giving the midships Honeywell a better line of fire, Raymond began cranking out the rounds with a dull metallic "thunk, thunk, thunk, thunk."

Morelly rolled over and stuck his head around the wall in time to see the high explosive shells begin to land across the entire tree line. Trees and foliage shook and spat dirt as each of the evenly spaced rounds struck a foreign object and detonated. So thick was the foliage, however, that when the smoke and dirt died away, that portion of the jungle immediately assumed its previously untouched façade. But hostile fire stopped coming from each position in the vicinity of a grenade blast and that was all that mattered for the time being.

Morelly prepared to hoist Mendez and begin a sprint for the boat when he saw five uniformed North Vietnamese emerge from behind the hootch. Perhaps they had witnessed the grenades' devastation, felt their time was coming and elected to attempt to salvage their ambush. Four held automatic rifles at the hip while the fifth brandished a loaded rocket launcher. Morelly popped up from behind the wall and squeezed off a burst in their direction. One man buckled over and collapsed while a second spun and fell against the hootch wall. He quickly recovered his feet in an instant of pure reflex action, then pitched forward. The rocket man had been taking aim at the PBR but now he swung his long pipe with the pointed, bulbous charge at its business end toward the wall and fired.

Morelly caught a glimpse of the white fiery tail flashing through the air and he fell to the ground behind the wall. His pushed himself into the rubble for protection but instinctively reached out with one hand to try to cover the pilot's head. He screamed a warning but was drowned out by a deafening roar, so loud that he did not even hear it. He felt the impact shake the wall and slam his head down into the ground.

On the boat, McGinn quickly trained on target and cut down the rocket man with his first burst. Raymond had no time to go back to his M-60 so he continued to crank out grenade rounds, trying to place them short of the men to cause shrapnel wounds. One round struck the corner of the hootch, detonated and knocked one gunner to the ground. He rolled over once and rose to his knees, only to be caught and flipped backward by McGinn's fifty-caliber rounds.

The one remaining soldier had expended his ammunition and stood staring starkly. A grenade round struck him directly in the lower leg, somersaulting him forward. His foot and bits of leg dispersed with the dirt and grass into the air. He landed limply on the ground, lying there only a split second until McGinn found him with his machine guns. The body twitched and rolled as though being driven by a powerful firehose.

Nearly half the wall seemed to have fallen atop Morelly and the other two men. He raised his head and pulled himself out of the rubble. His left arm felt slightly numb and blood trickled into his mouth. The rocket's shrapnel had taken several fairly large chunks and many small nicks out of his arm. The left side of his flak jacket was hanging in shreds, the charred white fiberglass protruding from gashes in the green nylon covering. He wiped blood from his neck and knew he had been hit there also, although he felt nothing. Partly adrenaline, partly shock, he analyzed almost remotely.

He looked about and knew immediately that Mendez was dead. Either by choice or by chance, the unfortunate little spy had ended up face down on top of a rock outcropping that had left his body just slightly more exposed than Morelly or the pilot when the rocket struck. His back had caught a great deal of shrapnel, which blew his shirt and the seat of his pants away and tore deeply into his skin. His arms and legs were still cased in tattered green fatigue, but that was all that remained identifiable. The torso was just a bleeding pile of meat. Morelly seized one of Mendez' arms, half expecting to pull it straight out of its socket, and wrestled the body off the rocks and onto the ground. The pilot scrambled to his knees and backed away, gazing down at the gruesome sight of what remained of Mendez.

"You all right?" Morelly asked.

"Yeah. I guess so."

"You were lucky."

"Christ, do we take him back?" He grabbed the other

arm as though preparing to drag the corpse back to the boat.

"Got to. He's really fucked up, though. We gotta . . ."

"Lieutenant, he's a civilian," the pilot stammered.

"He's an American, pal. Let's go. We gotta be careful and try to drag him all in one piece."

Morelly turned away and motioned his boat's guns silent. Then for several seconds he waited, listening. Beyond the PBR's idling engines he heard nothing. He was startled momentarily as a single M-60 round exploded, cooked off by the heat built up in the chamber of Raymond's weapon.

"Hagren," he called.

"Sir."

"Rake the tree line for ten seconds. Just the trees. Don't hit the bodies."

"Roger that."

Immediately the din of the boat's machine guns rose up again. The sweet blue-white smoke from the boat's guns wafted gently over the men hunkered down behind the wall. For ten seconds Morelly could barely hear himself think as several hundred rounds whizzed overhead. He applied all his concentration to the lifelessly contorted forms that lay beside the hootch.

"Lemon," he called when the firing had ceased. "Come here. Hurry up. You guys cover him."

Without a word Lemon was off the boat, zigzagging his way to the wall.

"OK, Lemon. We're going to see if any of those slopes are alive. I want to find out what the hell the story is here."

"Right, sir."

"What's your name?" Morelly finally asked the pilot, over his shoulder.

"Denson. Jim Denson."

"And you really are a freaking pilot after all?"

"That's affirm."

Morelly nodded. "At least something came out right today. OK, let's go check 'em out. Among the three of us we should be able to get one back to the boat if there's one still alive. Hagren," Morelly called over his shoulder, "we're going to check the bodies. Cover us."

"Roger. We gotcha."

Two of the men were destroyed beyond question. Morelly moved to the third body and knelt beside it. He pushed the head to one side with his rifle butt and was met by a cold stare. "These bastards are all dead."

"No, sir," Lemon said. "This one here's alive. He's breathing. Really in bad shape though."

Denson quickly examined the one remaining soldier. "Here's one that's still kicking." He rolled the man onto his back, exposing a gaping shoulder and chest wound. The delirious head rocked back and forth in shock.

"Yeah, he'll do," Morelly said. "Is that one conscious, Lemon?"

"I'm not sure, sir."

Morelly moved to the man's side and poked the rifle muzzle into his ribs. An arm moved down to cover the point of pain. "Yeah, he's OK. Let's get 'em both to the boat."

With assistance from Raymond, both soldiers were quickly dragged aboard. "Leave 'em here on the engine covers," Morelly ordered. "Price, get Mr. Denson a flak jacket from below. Hag, these guys are North Vietnamese regulars. They're not local VC."

"Yessir. You knew that when they stepped out there to take us on. Crazy motherfuckers. Mac, you get re-armed up there." McGinn waved over his head and began climbing out of his mount, pulling two one-hundred-round cans of fifty-caliber ammunition with him. "We ready to move, sir?"

"Yeah. Let's get the hell out of here. Oh, shit! We almost forgot Mendez, lyin' out there. Raymond, come on. We gotta drag Mendez back to the boat. Grab a poncho."

They rolled the remains of Mendez into a poncho that they then more or less slid up onto the bow, wedging the body between McGinn's circular gun tub and the boat's forward superstructure. Hagren gunned the engines astern but the boat merely shuddered. Morelly bent down and poked his head into the Flat. The rpm's were struggling to rise. Hagren banged his throttles to full ahead then back to full astern in a futile attempt to blow the pumps clear.

"Fuckin' grass and shit in the pumps. Lemon, get on the pumps. Hurry up. Starboard first."

Morelly stood momentarily still as he watched Lemon claw his way into the strangling pumps. "Denson, here I'll take my .38 back. Get on that M-60 and cover the tree line there. Price, let's get these guys set up against the gunwale."

"Yessir."

One of the Vietnamese was obviously feeling the pain but his comrade, in shock, hung on to the thin edge of consciousness. Raymond bent down beside Morelly. "We ain't gonna get much outta these guys."

"I want to know if there are more of them waiting for us down the canal."

"Nothing we can do about it if there are. Ain't no other way out."

"I know."

"You don't speak zip."

"Not a whole hell of a lot, you're right." Morelly shook the more alive of the two to get his attention. The growing look of fear in both men's eyes told Morelly they were beginning to realize where they were. "OK, *Ohm*. Where are the rest of your pals? Where are the Viet Cong? *Viet Cong di dau?*"

Heads lolled, eyes rolled. One of the soldiers began to gurgle up blood. Both were sweating profusely.

"Hey, motherfucker, *Viet Cong di dau?*"

While one of the two continued to roll his head back and forth, his eyes seemed to show more alertness. Morelly was sure that he was now conscious enough to know what was going on. But he said nothing. Morelly repeated the question twice more, then pulled out his .38 and cocked it in the man's face.

"Price, get back there and help Lemon clean the pumps." Morelly needed some privacy.

"Yessir."

"OK, fucker." He seized the man by the throat and held the pistol inches from his eyes. "Now one more time."

A series of low moans came from the mouth that was beginning to bleed more heavily. The man's fear was showing clearly, but he did not want to communicate. Morelly grabbed the other soldier, still semi-conscious, held him up for a second, then pushed him over the gunwale into the canal. As he popped briefly to the surface, sputtering and choking, Morelly finished him with one shot from his .38.

"Now, you little bastard," he said, turning back to his remaining captive. "That's going to happen to you if you don't start telling me where the fuck the VC are. *Viet Cong di dau?*"

"*No biet . . . no biet . . .*" The eyes were glazing over but still comprehending.

"We got 'em, Mr. Morelly," Raymond panted, climbing up onto the engine covers, both sleeves wet from working inside the Jacuzzi pumps. "Hag, you're clean. Light 'em off."

"This guy's nowhere," Morelly hissed through his teeth.

"Sir?"

"Nowhere. This guy's saying nothing."

"You want me to tie him up in the stern?"

"No. We got enough problems."

The boat moved off the bank and into midstream. Hagren slammed the throttles back and forth, turning the craft on the proverbial dime as he got it moving down the canal in a matter of seconds.

Morelly stood, pulled his M-16 off the canopy top and changed magazines. "Roll him overboard."

Raymond grabbed the man by the back of his shirt and began to push him over the gunwale. One thin hand seized Raymond's ankle while the other held onto the railing. With an effort, Raymond finally loosed the surprisingly strong grip and the man disappeared into the wake. He reappeared almost instantly. Morelly raised his weapon to his shoulder but, at the last second, did not fire. He was not sure why. Enough insanity for one day?

Raymond shook his head. "You didn't want to do that, Mr. Morelly. I know you didn't. But, man, you know Goddamned well, he'd kill you in a heartbeat if he had the chance. You shoulda let me do it. I woulda shot the little fucker for you."

"It's OK, Price."

"Well, he's done anyway. Let him drown in this Goddamn canal."

"Yeah. Where's the flak jacket for Denson?"

"Oh, shit. I'm sorry." He slid two green vests off the canopy. "Here you go, Mr. Denson. One for you too Mr. Morelly. That one's had it. You hurt bad?"

Morelly broke the cylinder out of his .38 and ejected the empty casings onto the brass-littered deck. "I don't think so."

"Well, you could use a battle dressing. Lemme see can't I find that Goddamn first aid kit somewhere."

SEVENTEEN

With both pumps running full power, Hagren maneuvered the boat into midstream and gunned it forward, pushing the throttles hard ahead to full speed.

"Lansing, this is Victor . . . Goddamn radios!" Morelly cursed, realizing the mike was dead in his hand. He ducked around the Flat and down into Chief's Quarters, flicking on the battle lantern as he did. The primary radio had two bullet holes through it. Bad day for radios. The secondary still appeared to be functioning, however, and he flicked it over to primary frequency, changing the numbers on the tens and digits dials from 55.05 to 45.10.

"Lansing, this is Victor," he said after establishing contact with Franklin at Tra Cu. "We have broken off contact at this time. Ambush by ground force appeared to be planned. We got one friendly KIA and one radio

| 157

dead. We're coming out and we need air cover and 714 at the end of the canal to meet us."

"Roger. Understood. 714 is underway and two boats have been scrambled from here. It'll take those two about one five minutes to get there. 714 will be there ASAP. I'll get the air up right away."

"Roger, out."

"If they were back there, and if they planned to hit us, they're gonna be along here, too," Hagren said, looking straight ahead, concentrating on keeping exactly in midstream.

"I know. Mr. Denson, come here a minute." Denson stepped off the engine covers onto the deck beside the Flat.

"There's an M-16 and an M-79 in there. A twelve-gauge too. Take what you want. There's ammo down below."

"Right."

"Did you know those guys were there?'

"Yeah. I had some local VC pushing me around for the past few days. Then last night, or real early this morning, I guess, they moved me near here and met up with a force of NVA regulars. I don't know how large the NVA force was because I was blindfolded most of the time. They seemed to argue a lot for quite awhile, then the NVA took me and the VC disappeared. They brought me to that hootch and staked me out and while they were setting that swinging booby trap, the leader, I guess he was, told me they were using me for bait. He spoke pretty bad English, but he knew all the clichés. They had made fools of the Americans and had gotten 20,000 pi-asters for my release. Now they were going to kill the

Americans who came to save me, then they were going to kill me."

"Try 200,000 piasters," Morelly said, shaking his head. "So no matter what happens, the worst the VC can do is still have 180,000 for themselves. The zips must have lied when they ran into the NVA. Told them they were only getting 20,000 for the guy and had planned to ambush the Americans all along, but the NVA could have the glory of doing it.

"It wouldn't make any difference to the VC who came out on top in the fight. If the NVA were wiped out, the VC wouldn't have to split their money with anyone. If the NVA came to collect after they whacked us, the VC would hand over the 20,000 and still keep 180,000 for themselves."

The question of whether the entire ambush had been planned from the start by the Communists was purely academic and not worth consideration. The only man upon whom Morelly could have placed blame for the incident was Mendez, and he was no longer worth consideration either.

"Lansing Victor, this is Seawolf five-one. Do you read?"

"Roger, Seawolf, I copy."

"Roger, we're airborne at this time. I'm about zero seven out of your location. What's your exact position at this time?"

Morelly's heart sank. In seven minutes it would all be over for the boat and his crew, one way or the other. They couldn't sit where they were, that was for damn sure.

"He asked for our posit, sir," Hagren said.

"Five-one, I am about four klicks up the Tan Trang Canal moving west toward the Vam Co Dong."

"Roger, thank you, copy," came the calm, vibrating reply.

"That's one fucked-up arm you got there, sir," Hagren noted as he completed pushing his throttles to top speed. "Raymond, quick get the first aid kit and put a dressing on Mr. Morelly's arm here."

"I was lookin', Boats, I was lookin'," Raymond replied. "I can't find the fuckin' kit anywhere."

"In the small arms locker."

"That's a hell of a place for it."

Morelly had barely heard this exchange of remarks. His mind was further down the canal, trying to guess what the NVA had planned for them for the rest of the short trip. The band that had kept Denson and set up the PBR could conceivably have been simply a small cell, but Morelly doubted it. The Tan Trang Canal that far off the main river was acknowledged to be Indian country. It was an area where the VC and NVA could move about freely with little fear of interference. These areas were pockets of undeniable enemy control within a countrywide network of contested farmland and villages. So even if the initial action did involve only a small group, there could easily have been another totally unrelated enemy force in the area that could respond to the sounds of what were obviously Americans engaging the Communists. If these enemy soldiers happened to be Viet Cong, they could elect to move away from the action. On the other hand, if there was a North Vietnamese unit of eager regulars in the area, they could well be expected to search out a fight.

Morelly tried to concentrate on the water and the

banks that sped by on either side but somehow he found his mind drifting off. He began to think about being home and almost smiled. He did not smile because he remembered, as he often did when he dreamed of home, that there was no home. To him, home had been his room at Navy OCS in Newport, Rhode Island. It had been his bunk room on the USS Chara, the old-but-still-top-notch ammunition ship where he had done his first tour of Vietnam duty, offshore. After that, it was his apartment in Vallejo, California, where he had spent ten weeks learning how to command one of these little boats and keep it and himself out of situations such as the one in which he currently found himself. Still, he somehow always felt better when he thought of home. In fact, he probably felt happier thinking about home than a lot of men did when they thought about homes they actually had. They were stuck with reality. Morelly could make home be whatever and wherever he wanted it to be. Right at the moment, he wanted it to be acres of green grass and tall trees. And he would sit out in the sunshine of a quiet Sunday morning. Perhaps sit out on his stone patio and savor a Bloody Mary and a pair of eggs Benedict. That would be nice, he thought, as a stab of pain brought him back to the Coxswain's Flat.

"Sorry, sir. You OK?"

"Yeah, Price, thanks. Got it now?"

"Yeah, man, it'll do long's you don't go gettin' it shot off or nothin'. You lost a little blood. Shit, this whole thing's fucked up. Where's the Seawolves?"

"Won't be here for a few minutes yet."

"Jesus Christ. Few minutes and they might as well not . . ."

Raymond left the sentence unfinished and leaped to

his gun mount the instant he saw the straw floating in midstream directly in the path of the boat.

"Both banks," Morelly said almost without thinking. "They're going to stop us and hit us from both banks." He did not need to think. He had primed his mind with every possibility that he could imagine and he had beaten his brain into grasping and holding his planned response to any situation. Now, at the instant of crisis, he could open his mind, allow the situation to register and have the response action automatically pour forth. He had never encountered straw and had heard of its being used only once: against River Division 554 way over on the Grand Canal.

554 had gone into the canal with three PBRs. It happened only a couple of weeks after Morelly and his PBR class from San Francisco had arrived in country. The Executive Officer of 554, a Lieutenant named John Callard, had gone through PBR school with Morelly and was leading the patrol. It was a dark night and they had not seen the straw on the water. The boats ran directly into it and the Jacuzzi pumps proceeded to suck it up at a rapid rate until the pumps of all but the last boat were jammed full enough to keep water from being allowed out of the jets. With the boats dead in the water, the VC opened up with rocket and machine gun fire so intense that both lead boats were sunk almost before the crew could bring any fire of their own to bear. Callard and four other sailors were killed outright and another died in the medevac chopper. No one on the lead boats escaped without serious wounds. Fortunately, helicopters were in the air and moved in quickly to support the rescue efforts of the one remaining PBR.

As a vision of John Callard being blown through the

Coxswain's Flat fled through his head, Morelly became aware of Hagren, wrestling with both wheel and throttles to bring the boat to a halt. Realizing that they were damned if they stopped and damned if they didn't, Morelly hopped to the engine covers, picked up his M-16 and brought it to his shoulder.

"H and I both banks," he called as he squeezed the trigger and began putting bursts of fire randomly into the tree lines just ahead. Their best chance would be to try and gain some slight degree of benefit from seizing the opportunity to initiate fire, even though there were no active targets. Harassment and Interdiction fire was a common and useful tactic used, Morelly felt, altogether too infrequently lately as the number of Free Fire Zones became fewer and fewer. On more than one occasion, H&I fire had caused the VC to prematurely initiate an ambush that might have otherwise been successful, given adequate time to prepare and set it up.

The machine gun staccato rose almost immediately to a deafening pitch as Raymond and then Lemon opened fire on the north bank and McGinn pounded the south. Morelly expended and turned to pick up a second magazine from the canopy top when he realized Denson standing behind him, M-16 in hand, watching Raymond work out.

"That side, the south bank. Cover the south bank."

Denson jumped as though he had been stung. With a quick glance at Morelly, he swung toward the north bank and kept swinging until he faced south. Then he opened fire.

And so did the North Vietnamese. The fact that most of the fire was coming from further downstream indicated that the boat had avoided moving into the heart of the ambush. Nevertheless, there was enough to keep everyone busy. Yet Morelly knew that remaining where they were, dead in the water, could lead to nothing but disaster. Tracers flew back and forth between the boat and both sides of the canal.

A rocket flamed overhead from the north and detonated on the south bank among a group of muzzle flashes. Killing their own . . . well, that was a nice shot, Charlie, thought Morelly. A second rocket detonated on the water's surface directly off the starboard beam, blowing water and fragments into the boat. Raymond hunched over quickly, lowering his helmeted head like a football player about to meet a tackler head-on. He seized his left arm as fragments bit at it. He took one quick glance at the oozing bicep and continued to fire.

"One engine," Morelly called into the Flat. "We'll run on one engine at a time!"

Hagren pulled the air cutoff and choked the port diesel to death. "Tell Lemon to get the port. Now."

"Right. Denson, get back there and man the fifty."

"But I don't . . ."

"You'll figure it out in a hurry. You pull the trigger 'til it's empty."

Both Morelly and Denson moved behind Raymond and jumped down onto the pump covers.

"We're gonna run on one engine at a time," Morelly screamed at Lemon over the racket. "Denson'll take over the fifty. Start cleaning the port pump."

Lemon obediently scrambled around the machine gun and began knocking off the dog clamps that held the pump cover to the deck. This done, he hopped into the guts of the boat. Standing ankle deep in bilge water, he hunched over the pump itself to work at a large circular metal plug. It would have to come out before he could get his hands inside the Jacuzzi and begin working at the straw.

"Keep your head down," Denson called as he swung the machine gun's long barrel to the port side, directly over Lemon's back, and opened fire. Lemon did not acknowledge, but there was no doubt that he had gotten the message as he slapped his bare right arm when one of the hot shell casings bounced against his skin. His eardrums felt as though they would burst from the hammering explosions right over his head.

After some struggling he managed to free the plug and began pulling the straw out of the pump grates. Within forty seconds the pump was clean. He slammed the plug in place and called for Hagren to switch engines.

For the next few endless minutes, Lemon moved frantically from starboard pump to port pump and back to starboard as each one in turn would begin to run then immediately seize up, full of straw. During these minutes PBR 716 made no more than two or three knots and hostile fire continued to assault them, although considerably slackened in intensity. After the initial onslaught and heavy fire, the North Vietnamese had evidently pulled back to the security of their mud and stone bunkers, which lined the banks just behind the tree lines. Morelly expected they would be reloading and preparing for one final thrust before the boat could clear the canal mouth.

"You're clean," Lemon called out. "Both pumps are clean. Light off the port."

The engine roared to life alongside the already-straining starboard motor and the boat immediately began to rise out of the water, again capable of running all out. It seemed to gain more speed than it had ever had, possibly because of the now-lightened ammunition load, possibly because it sensed the end of its ordeal and was calling on every last ounce of energy that remained within its riddled fiberglass.

EIGHTEEN

McGinn caught several fleeting shapes moving behind the trees on the north bank further down the canal and took them under fire. Hagren was running at full speed now and, with the targets being just a bit ahead of the boat, only McGinn in the forward mount could bring any real firepower to bear on them. Nevertheless, when he opened up both Raymond and Denson began firing randomly at the now-quiet south bank. Morelly leaned over the canopy top to place a burst of M-16 fire into the tree line just ahead of where McGinn was concentrating.

His fears were being realized, for when McGinn saw soldiers moving from their original positions to new cover further downstream in the boat's path, Morelly knew immediately that they were preparing for another attack. As he emptied his magazine into the tree line, it all began again.

Three rockets zoomed simultaneously from amid the

foliage on the canal bank toward the boat. One passed overhead and another fell astern. "Don't know how to lead a moving target," Morelly thought, at the instant the third rocket struck the starboard side squarely, just above the waterline. The explosion threw Morelly off the engine covers, down into the Flat at Hagren's feet. Before he could pull himself up, Denson collapsed on top of him, unmoving. Pushing and pulling frantically, Morelly finally freed himself from the body from whose mouth vague, small sounds were being emitted. Evidently Denson was at least alive, which was more than Morelly knew about any of his crewmen.

As he got to his knees and pulled himself onto the engine covers, he saw Raymond lying at the base of his machine gun mount, rolling back and forth in a daze but otherwise apparently unhurt save for the previously in-flicted arm wound. The M-60's ammunition belt lay draped over his legs, blown from the breach by the force of the explosion that left the weapon itself twisted and torn in its swivel. Bits and pieces of the frail Honeywell littered the deck although the weapon's stock remained in its mount.

As he tried to stand, Morelly realized that his left leg would not hold the weight and he quickly looked down to find the lower half of his trousers missing. He could see nothing through the blood that began to fill his left boot. He reached down, feeling his leg section by section until he jabbed the palm of his hand unintentionally on a jagged protrusion of splintered bone. He realized that his calf was not completely intact. There was a section about the size of a small fist missing from the back of it, leaving the ripped bone exposed. He thought it strange that this had happened to him and yet he was not alto-

gether wildly upset about it as he had always dreamed he
would be if ever seriously wounded.

He looked up at Raymond who had now stopped
rolling around and was staring straight into Morelly's
eyes. Behind Raymond, Morelly could see Lemon apparently moving slowly, although it couldn't be too
slowly the way his flak jacket bounced with every step
and his helmet popped off his head, off his shoulder, and
then overboard into the boat's white wake. No, Morelly
thought dazedly, he was really moving pretty fast. And
he was calling to Raymond. Just as he reached Raymond's
position, he stopped. Hagren screamed something in the
background that brought Morelly at least partially back
to reality. He was about to answer Hagren when he realized what had happened to Lemon. The forward mo-
mentum of his rush to Raymond's side had been abruptly
halted as a bullet tore into his shoulder, nearly ripping
the arm from its socket. His body twisted halfway around
and seemed to hang in midair until caught by a second
bullet, which struck just at the base of the neck and blew
the boy's face away. The body crumpled out of sight, off
the engine covers, down onto the pump covers in the
stern.

"Fuck!" Raymond screamed as he saw Lemon's body
fall. He began to crawl forward toward the Flat, away
from the pump covers. "Fuck! Fuck! God, his head!"

Morelly moved as best he could and met him, pushing him backwards. "The after fifty, Price. You gotta get
on the after fifty."

"But he's layin' back there."

"Your 60's gone. We need the fire. Get back there."

There was no verbal answer. Their eyes met again

and held for an instant, then Raymond nodded and began to scramble toward the stern.

For the first time in many long seconds, Morelly stood, supporting himself on one leg and holding onto the stanchion that supported the canopy.

"I got one engine and I'm losing rpm's on that," Hagren called over his shoulder. Morelly looked at Hagren, noticing that the back of his neck was riddled with small gobs of blood caused by exploding fiberglass from the last hit. The boat was now moving slowly, laboriously, on one engine. Morelly glanced at the rpm indicators. The starboard one read zero, the port something under 2,000.

"Clearing up there on the south. Make for it and beach." He picked up the radio. "Seawolf, Seawolf, this is Lansing Victor. We're goin' down so we're gonna beach. South bank about one klick from the river. The area's very hot. I repeat, it'll be a hot LZ."

Through the static and bursting percussion of McGinn's still-firing machine guns, Morelly could barely make out a reply.

"Roger, hot LZ. I have . . . sight . . . time . . . I say again . . . you in sight . . . zero two . . ."

"Understand zero two minutes. Roger, we'll be on the bank."

"Ro . . . er. Understood . . . out."

Through the haze of smoke rising from the forward mount, Morelly saw two airborne shapes coming toward him, a few hundred feet above the trees. Hagren began to turn the wheel and inch the crippled boat toward the south side of the canal. Sporadic rocket and machine gun fire continued to assault the boat. Between the bursts fired by the boat's gunners, NVA rounds would ping here and there. A few rounds walked right across the canopy over Morelly and Hagren's heads, ripping the rubberized canvas, pinging off the stanchions, but never touching either of them. Something hit the radar dome over their heads and Morelly heard it issue a muffled explosion. Pieces of metal and plastic fell onto the canopy. A round pinged off the stanchion right next to Morelly's head and ricocheted through the top of the right shoulder of his flak jacket, never touching him.

Red and white tracers arched across the river from both sides, although most of the fire was now coming from the north where the tree line ran along unbroken, as it did not on the south. McGinn had swiveled his mount at a hand signal from Hagren. Realizing what was happening, he concentrated his fire on either side of the clearing toward which Hagren was heading, trying to force any NVA soldiers in the foliage to back away. Raymond had not been able, for one reason or another, to move Lemon's body from the port pump covers where it had fallen, so he had no choice but to stand on the starboard covers and fire to port—to the south. Thus the boat was bringing no fire to bear on the north bank and hostile fire from that side was becoming more accurate.

All around Hagren and Morelly in the Coxswain's Flat, more bullets continued to zip, rip and ping as the North Vietnamese gunners tried especially hard to kill them, the two men at the boat's controls. One hit the canopy frame and bent it outward. Morelly stepped out of the Flat and promptly fell to the engine covers as his leg gave way. He knew he was losing too much blood.

He reached across Denson to the metal first aid box and tried to pull it open. His left hand wet with blood, his fingers slipped as he fumbled with the latch. He cut his index finger although he did not know it. Finally the box popped open just as it was supposed to do in such cases and Morelly ripped out a battle dressing, quickly unfolded it and wrapped it around his left calf.

This done he picked up the M-79 grenade launcher beside Denson's body, grabbed a bandolier of rounds from the gun rack and twisted around toward the north bank. He could make out muzzle flashes clearly. They were no more than thirty yards away even as the boat neared the opposite bank. He began to pop off rounds as quickly as he could fire and reload the single-shot weapon. At times he would have a second round in the air before the first had yet hit its target.

Looking straight into the tracers and knowing he was the only gun returning fire, Morelly felt very alone in this, a situation where men cannot be drawn any more closely together.

"Raymond," he screamed. "You gotta get some fire on the other side! With me! With me!" He gestured wildly toward the north bank, over their stern. Raymond acknowledged and tried to swing around. He slipped in the blood and water in the stern, fell over Lemon's body, and slipped again. He held onto the fifty-caliber machine gun and pulled himself to his feet. He had one foot on the deck and the other on top of Lemon, but at least he could now fire into the north bank tree line, along with Morelly.

A rocket arched directly toward the boat. Morelly, unable to move to take cover, if there had been any cover on the fiberglass boat, hunched over and braced for the blast. Instead, the round fell short and spewed water over his head and down his neck. He looked up just as a second rocket was sent on its way, this time with more accuracy. The gunner had had a lucky angle. The rocket whooshed up the side of the boat and somehow found part of its bow just at the waterline, detonating inside the hull only a few feet from McGinn's legs as they hung exposed from his nylon-webbed seat in the gun tub. Normally, had the forward gunner cried out, Morelly would not have heard it from back aft for no human sound could be heard over the din of three fifty caliber machine guns. But McGinn ceased firing, seized the metal scarf ring in pain, and screamed. Morelly heard it. It stopped quickly. As if to make the pain go away or somehow diminish, McGinn groped for and found the firing handle once again and clenched the trigger mechanism tightly. Both weapons began firing a sustained volley, the tracers no longer on targets as they had so professionally been for the past few minutes. Instead they were flying wildly into the treetops.

As Morelly pumped off the last rounds of the bandolier of M-79 grenades, a hard jolt threw him nearly to the deck on top of Denson. They had reached the bank. Before he could move, however, Hagren was out of the Flat and beside him.

"You stand, sir?"

"Yes."

"We gotta get the hell off this boat. We're goin' down."

Morelly looked around to see that the stern was under water up to the top of the transom. Raymond was standing waist deep in water, firing the fifty into the trees across the river. Still sitting facing that side, Morelly could not tell if fire was being received from Raymond's target areas. He grabbed Hagren's shoulder and pulled himself up and over to the port side gunwale. Hagren stooped down, checked Denson briefly, then picked him up under the armpits and began dragging him up onto the engine covers.

"He's still alive."

Raymond depressed his machine gun trigger and took one last sweep through a 180-degree arc along the bank, then leaped out of the flooding water, up onto the engine covers. He spun around on his knees, plunged his arms back into the bloody water and dragged Lemon's body up onto the engine covers alongside himself. Morelly began to try to get to his feet, but everyone was knocked to the deck by the force of a rocket hit on the forward gun mount. This blast rocked the boat and nearly edged it off the canal bank. Recovering quickly, Morelly motioned for Raymond to move past him and drag Lemon's body forward.

"Into the water," Morelly screamed. "It's shallow. Into the water with Lemon and drag him ashore."

With a quick nod, Raymond simply rolled off the engine covers and over the side, like he did it every day. Impressive as that move was, he also somehow managed to hold onto part of Lemon's uniform and drag the body, like a heavy sack, with him. Hagren had exerted his great strength and had thrown Denson up onto the canopy, or what was left of it, and as Hagren walked forward on the gunwale, he moved Denson's body forward simply by sliding it across the canvas.

The rocket round that had just hit the forward gun tub had detonated just under McGinn's right machine gun and had blown the weapon completely off its mount. The heavy gun caromed off the boat's forward super-structure and into the water, sizzling. McGinn's flak jacket had been absolutely no help to him with the explosion being at chest height not twelve inches in front of him. The metal back plate against which he sat had withstood the blast, but his body had been flattened against it with incredible force. His head hung upside down over the back of the plate and one arm lay over the side of the tub, in the mass of splattered nylon, fiberglass and metal. The other arm smoked and burned sickeningly as it rested on the remaining red-hot machine gun barrel. As he dragged Denson by, Hagren kicked the arm off the barrel and stopped to pick up the M-16 that McGinn always kept nearby.

Morelly was now alone in the sinking stern of the boat. He would be the last one off. He put his arm down to try to get some leverage somewhere to raise himself off the deck. His hand found an M-16 rifle stock instead. He pulled the weapon to him, and set it vertically on the tilting deck, barrel down. He used it as a crutch to lift himself up. He leaned against the splinter shield. On the opposite bank a group of three NVA, emboldened and smelling blood when they saw the boat beach itself, began to move out of the tree line, down toward the water, to get better lines of fire.

Morelly pulled up his "crutch," balanced himself against the splinter shield of the Coxswain's Flat, and cut them all down with a burst that expended the M-16's magazine. He dropped the weapon to the deck and, holding onto the canopy stanchion to steady himself, got ready to try to jump, with one foot, up onto the engine covers. The PBR's American flag caught his eye. It had been rolled up around its short flagstaff, and stowed on the starboard-side inboard bulkhead in a gun rack just a couple of feet away. Time seemed to stand still.

He reached out, lifted the flagstaff out of the rack, and desperately hurried to unwrap it. His hands were shaking. His leg was burning. Two bullets, from somewhere, plowed into the molded fiberglass of the forward superstructure, just beside him. Yet another pinged off something metallic nearby. He ripped his K-bar knife from its sheath and cut the flag away from its flagstaff. He stuffed it into one of his cargo pockets.

He reached up to the canopy stanchion overhead and used it to leverage himself up onto the engine covers. He then began to move forward, up the gunwale, toward the bank. He passed the forward gun tub. The first thing he saw was McGinn's head, hanging upside-down over the back of his seatback. He picked up the boy's arm by the wrist, as if to try to begin dragging him off the boat. It was amazingly light. He lifted it up, and nothing was attached. There was no body attached to the arm.

Morelly fought back tears in his eyes and bile in his throat. He knew he would have to violate one of the cardinal rules of the river: he would have to leave McGinn's body behind, to be retrieved later. He was frozen. For the first time in the fight, he was frozen and had no idea what to do next.

"Sir!" He heard Hagren scream. "Come on! Get off the boat!"

"McGinn . . ." Morelly called, somewhat blankly.

"Get a tag! Get a tag! Come on. We're gonna die here."

Morelly snapped to. He reached down. There was almost no neck to search. But in a second he found them—both dog tags, chains and all. He ripped off the lower tag and, as gently as he could under the circumstances, put the other one into McGinn's mouth, per protocol. Finally, he picked up McGinn's camo bandana, torn and red with blood, and quickly stuffed it into his other cargo pocket.

He took one last look around. A twelve-gauge shotgun lay on the deck. Morelly picked it up. It was partially wedged under a poncho. Mendez. Morelly had forgotten totally about Mendez's body, wrapped in the poncho. It was all almost too much to take in. Now weakened and on his knees, he crawled forward and fell off the boat, to the muddy bank. As he did, several rounds, meant for him, laced into the bow of the boat, shredding more fiberglass and pinging off the aluminum.

"What about Mac, sir? And the spook?" Hagren panted as Morelly joined him, exhausted, behind the protection of a small hump of mud along the bank.

"We'll come back for McGinn. No. Sturgis will be able to get him. And the spook. We got all we can take care of right here."

At the far end of the small clearing, against a scrawny tree line, three hootches sat huddled together. Otherwise there was no sign of life. Hagren rolled onto his back to survey the scene across the canal.

"They all shut up, sir. What the fuck . . ."

"It's the helos. Must be the helos," Morelly said. As he spoke, the welcome beating clatter of the two Navy hueys reached their ears from behind the treetops. Simultaneously, in the distance downstream, a lone PBR, no doubt Sturgis, streamed into sight, kicking up white water on both sides as it sped up the canal.

NINETEEN

The first helicopter, the Fire Team Leader, swept in low over the trees and overflew the beached PBR and the clearing to recon the situation into which he would be landing. The trail ship remained higher, lagging behind the Leader, poised to provide covering fire. Behind Morelly now he heard the "bap, bap, bap" of the Fire Team Leader's rotor blades as the chopper made a steep banking turn prior to commencing his landing approach into the clearing.

Morelly painfully rolled over against the mud hump and watched the huey pull out of its turn, level off and begin to move, more slowly now, across the canal toward the clearing. As it did so, a large box dropped out of each side of the chopper—the gunners discarding excess ammunition from their M-60 door guns in order to lighten up for the passengers. As the chopper passed over the water, the north bank erupted once again. White and red tracers arched lazily up at the helicopter. It seemed to move so slowly, so ponderously, and the tracers arched through the sky almost beautifully.

The Leader had already passed over the Communist positions so he had no opportunity to return fire. In fact, the pilot probably had no idea he was receiving fire except that the trail ship would surely give him the word via radio. Morelly guessed that the Seawolves were also in radio communication with Sturgis, for as the PBR neared the scene, the trail ship pulled out of what appeared to be the commencement of a firing run on the north bank and swung instead back to the south to cover the landing. As this maneuver was executed, Sturgis's boat raced between the remains of PBR 716 and the hostile north bank and poured suppressive fire into the entire tree line.

The beating blades kicked up what little dust there was on the edge of the canal as they carried the aircraft over the sinking boat and into the clearing. Its nose began pulling up as the pilot prepared to set down. Door gunners on both sides leaned far out over the landing skids, watching the ground through giant black goggles, machine guns at the ready.

"Let's try and give 'em some cover fire if they need it," Morelly said to no one in particular.

As the helo inched downward, the pilot swung the tail boom to the east so that the ship began to settle to the ground broadside between the hootches and the five men. As the skids touched down, the nearest door gunner shifted his weapon to one hand and began waving urgently to the men who had begun to climb from behind the mud hump and make their way across the open ground. Hagren was dragging Denson and Raymond was carrying Lemon, fireman's carry. Morelly limped behind them. As they began to move, the three hootches came to life with small arms fire.

Rounds began to kick up around the helicopter as the small group made their way all too slowly across the twenty yards of naked terrain.One door gunner had put down his weapon and was frantically trying to disconnect his radio wire. He was about to jump out and come help them, but he fell backward as the aircraft violently shifted position on the ground, rose slightly, fell hard and rose again, this time high into the air. The rotors whined. Morelly could see the pilot struggling with the controls, one foot hanging under his seat instead of on the pedal where it should have been.

A large section of the "greenhouse" on the underside of the helicopter was badly shot up. The clear Plexiglas greenhouse formed the forward portion of the huey's underbelly. Through it the pilot could look down, between his feet, and see the upcoming ground when he was making a landing. The pilot had been hit in the foot or leg and was losing control. Morelly could see the damage clearly as the chopper careened upward, away from the clearing, into the sky. He could see the co-pilot struggling with the controls. The pilot was now sideways in his seat, helmet back, hands gripping his wounded leg.

Hagren quickly expended his M-16 on the hootches. As he did so, the trail ship swept high overhead and dived toward the enemy. With a series of whooshing blasts, the pilot punched off what must have been fully half of his fourteen 2.75-inch rockets. As they struck the ground, Morelly realized that several of the rockets were fiery white phosphorous.

The hootches disintegrated under the intense heat. Everything—even the dirt, it seemed—burned and crackled viciously. Two men rolled from one hootch. Both of them were on fire. One was totally enveloped in flame and staggered no more than five feet from the blaze before collapsing, motionless. The second man fell to the ground and rolled in the dust, desperately trying to smother the flames that clung to his back. Did he know, as Morelly did, that there was no way to put out a white phosphorous fire? That it would burn until it had no more fuel left to nourish it? The man was no more than thirty feet away and Morelly would have liked to kill him. He raised the shotgun, but held his fire. The man ceased thrashing and in a matter of seconds became still, nearly unidentifiable as a human being.

The lead ship circled once after the rocket strike, apparently with the co-pilot at the controls, and edged in once again to attempt a pickup. As it set down, both door gunners hopped out, trailing ammunition belts into the ship, and began to place H&I fire into the entire tree line. As they did, they received scattered and sporadic fire in return—erratic rounds, into the air, into the dirt.

Raymond reached the chopper first. He dumped Lemon's body in and then threw himself in. Hagren had dragged Denson, the pilot, up to the side of the helo and, with frantic adrenaline-fed strength, lifted Denson's body off the ground, much like a javelin thrower as he readies his tool, and threw him headfirst into the helicopter. The body landed crosswise against Raymond, who immediately scuttled to the far side, dragging the unconscious Denson with him.

Morelly limped up to the edge of the helo door and rolled himself in onto the vibrating metal floor. The door gunner beside him leaped back into the aircraft as well and immediately pressed the intercom button beneath

his helmet's mouthpiece as he nervously watched the back
of his mate who continued to blaze away on the opposite side. The firing gunner quickly got the message and
he backed into the opposite doorway, popping his ass up
onto the deck while cradling his hot machine gun just
off his lap.

Rapidly, the idling blades began to build revolutions
and Morelly could feel the first stirrings of the ship as it
became lighter and lighter in an effort to be airborne.
One of the gunners hit Morelly on the shoulder and
pointed to a set of headphones with microphone attached
that hung on the back of the pilot's seat. Morelly placed
the set on his head and caught the end of the pilot's transmission over the intercom.

" . . . not going to make it. We're not going to get
off like this. We must have taken a hit someplace. I can't
build full power."

The ship shook and rocked gamely, just barely too
heavy to fly. The gunners looked at each other blankly
for a second before one pressed his talk button. "We've
dumped everything. The extra ammo's gone. We can't
get any lighter."

For a moment there was silence as the line went dead
in Morelly's ears.

"Wait one. Wait a minute." One of the gunners
crawled up beside Morelly and reached past him to where
Denson lay. He took Denson's face in one gloved hand
and turned it toward his own. "One of these guys is dead."

Morelly grabbed the gunner's arm with one hand
and his talk button with the other. "He's unconscious.
He's out cold. He's not dead. We wouldn't have . . ."

"I'm sorry, Lieutenant," said the door gunner. "He's
gone. Look at his eyes." Morelly whipped around and

seized Denson by the shirt collar, shaking the body in an attempt to revive it. Denson stared back at him with dull, dead eyes.

For the first time, the pilot, wounded but coherent, spoke directly to Morelly over the intercom. "OK, Lieutenant, I'm sorry. We gotta put him out. We got another fire team and a flight of Apaches inbound. Someone'll pick him up with the other bodies."

Both gunners wrestled with Denson's lifeless body until they finally had it out the door. Just like that. Gone. Dumped back onto the battlefield, among the enemy against whom the patrol had risked everything to save him.

Exhausted, in shock and unable finally to either speak or move, Morelly, Hagren and Raymond just sat or lay sprawled on the huey's deck, immobile, watching, glazed over. Almost immediately the helo began to lift, leaving Denson, the reason for the entire disastrous mission, alone in the swirling dust of the clearing.

The huey was still only a few feet off the ground. NVA sniper rounds continued to arch up wildly from the trees below. One pinged off the partition between the pilots and the after section where the three men now sat on the bare aluminum deck. Another hit the doorframe with a glancing "beeeow" and a spark. A single NVA soldier leapt from hiding, AK-47 at his shoulder, and ripped off a long burst of fire. His rounds raked the helo from bottom to top. Morelly instinctively turned toward the fire and brought up his twelve-gauge. His first blast was short, kicking up the dirt. His second hit the soldier squarely in the chest and blew him back into the underbrush.

Morelly threw the empty shotgun out of the helo

and rolled back inside, away from the door. One round from the NVA's burst had hit Hagren. It was the kind of lucky shot that never seemed to catch up with you on a good day. Only when everything else was already going to hell.

Hagren said nothing and his face showed more surprise than anything else. His eyes betrayed an instant of fear, then went blank as he slumped over against the door gunner's leg. The gunner quickly set his machine gun against the rear firewall and bent over the body. He placed his hand over Hagren's chest, felt for a pulse, then checked the eyes.

The gunner looked up. He looked at Morelly, and pressed his intercom button. Morelly watched his mouth move. The voice came through Morelly's headphones. "Your man's dead, sir." The gunner's eyes locked onto Morelly's and he shook his head slightly. There was somehow, behind the helmet, the goggles and the microphone, an expression of true compassion, even in the heat of this desperate moment. A dead comrade was universally mourned. "I'm sorry, sir. I . . . I'm sorry." Morelly nodded his comprehension.

"Lieutenant," the pilot or co-pilot cut in, "You got a message we're supposed to pass to Lansing and Atlantic Island, that right?"

Morelly remembered "Bright Knight" but he had no energy or will left to even push his button and reply. His mission had failed. He looked at one of the gunners who understood.

"No sir. He's got no message right now."

"Roger that," the pilot answered flatly.

Morelly felt cold but his palms began to sweat as though he was burning up. Sweat on his forehead and upper lip was cold and his eyes began to water. He moved away from Hagren toward the open door on the opposite side of the helo. The cord on his headphones ran out and pulled the set off his head.

The countryside below was peaceful and lusciously green. Vietnam was a beautiful country. On the water, the small green figure of Sturgis's PBR was outlined in the white of its wake as it sped out of the Tan Trang Canal and turned onto the Vam Co Dong.

Morelly looked down and back. They were still only a few hundred feet off the ground. He could see their PBR 716, like a broken toy, stuck into the canal bank. Its stern end, all the way up to Hagren's Coxswain's Flat, was under water. At least Hagren didn't have to see that. The pieces of McGinn's body were no longer in and around his gun tub on the fore deck, and the poncho with Mendez inside was no longer there either. Sturgis and his crew had picked them up. Denson's body still lay in the clearing.

Morelly stared out into green foliage and blue sky. The wind whipped his face and he tried not to think about Hagren. Or about McGinn's burning arm or Lemon's exploding face or Denson lying in the dust of the rotor wash. But the harder he tried, the more vivid these scenes became. He could see them. And smell them. He leaned further out over the deck edge to catch more wind.

Although he did not want to, he looked around. Raymond was sitting straight upright, gazing at nothing as tears rolled down his cheeks.

Morelly's eyes settled on the full-open, dead stare on Hagren's face and he began to tremble violently. He seized the gunner's trouser leg for support, pushed his head out into the cold rushing air and began to vomit uncontrollably.

TWENTY

"Attention on deck!" the Chief Petty Officer bellowed in a loud and salty voice.

Most of the yeomen and young officers in the huge, wide open aluminum building, the size of two football fields side by side, shuffled to their feet and assumed modified positions of attention. Ensign George Arthur, obscure behind a large desk and five-foot-high partitions, chose instead to hunch over in his chair, out of view. It must have taken the stately Admiral a full minute or so to walk across the River Patrol Force headquarters building and enter the office of Captain McGinnis, the Force Commander or Commodore. At least it seemed like a hell of a long time to be hunched over. Arthur reprimanded himself for the childish avoidance of such menial ceremony. He realized it would have been more comfortable to stand than to be all bent up for so long.

"Carry on."

Arthur straightened up and looked at the wall clock across the building. Two minutes to nine. In about one minute, Captain McGinnis would escort the Admiral from his office to the Briefing Room where they and the multitude of Lieutenant Commanders who made up the Force staff would endure the daily morning briefing.

The briefings were generally so dull, in fact, that Arthur rarely attended even though they were an accepted means of avoiding about twenty minutes' work in the morning. Evidently Admiral White, overall commander of not just the PBRs but all Naval "assets" in the new Sea Lords theatre of operations in the Mekong Delta, felt the same way. Although his office was only a short jeep ride away in nearby Can Tho, he was almost never present for the briefings. The Admiral's "assets" included the PCFs or Swift Boats, the "heavies" or armored craft of the Mobile Riverine Force, Seawolf helicopter fire teams, the Seals, the Seabees, and so on in addition to the PBRs of the River Patrol Force. Sea Lords embraced operations that would become Navy lore throughout the Delta, like Tran Hung Dao, Barrier Reef, the Vinh Te Canal and Giant Slingshot.

Today was different and Arthur felt fairly certain he knew why. It had to do with the PBR that River Division 435 lost the day before up on Giant Slingshot, and with the manila folders that rested in front of him on his desk. The fine Binh Thuy dust that seeped through the screened windows beside his desk had already, in a matter of minutes, placed a covering of brown gritty particles on top of the top folder, marked "McGinn, Wayne A., B576-367, GMG-2, USN, River Division 435." Underneath McGinn's folder was one just like it for a Boatswain's Mate First Class named Hagren and a Boat Seaman named Lemon.

Arthur brushed off the top folder, then picked all three up and rubbed them across his thigh to make sure they were perfectly clean. He then put all three into his top desk drawer. As he did so he looked up to see Captain McGinnis, Admiral White and Commander Irwin, the Force Deputy Commander, making their way from McGinnis's enviously air-conditioned office (the only one on the base) to the Briefing Room. Arthur rose from his seat and walked across the floor. He felt certain that this briefing would not be as dull as usual.

Inside the Briefing Room a small, thin and prematurely balding Lieutenant Commander stood nervously behind a crudely lacquered plywood podium and toyed with a long wooden pointer. Behind him stretched a huge wall map, floor to ceiling, of the Mekong Delta including most of the Third and Fourth Corps Tactical Zones. In front of him, Admiral White was taking his seat in the middle of three chairs set up along the opposite side of the rectangular conference table. The Admiral picked up the white place card reading "CTF 194.9" and jammed it into his breast pocket. Captain McGinnis seated himself to the Admiral's right, Commander Irwin to the left. As they settled down the underlings, who in the Army would be called "horse holders," dropped unceremoniously onto the straight-backed chairs that lined the rear wall. For Arthur and two junior Lieutenants there were not enough chairs and they were forced to stand in a remote corner. With a nod from McGinnis, the briefing began.

"Good morning, Admiral. Captain. Commander. Gentlemen. There were seven incidents in the past twenty-four hours, three major and four minor. All but two of the actions took place in the lower Delta. I'll brief you first on the three major incidents.

"At 0620 yesterday, a drone minesweeper attached to River Division 535 was destroyed by a mine of unknown type at point '1' in the Vinh Te Canal."

The little man left his script and the podium and moved across the floor to point to the red number "1" stuck onto the Vinh Te Canal, just on the Vietnam side of the Cambodian border. He then stuttered slightly as he started to speak again, but recovered his poise as he regained the security of his podium.

"The drone was unmanned at the time . . . uh . . . of course . . . and as I said, was being operated electronically from a Division 535 PBR about one hundred yards astern. The drone was totally destroyed and sank immediately. Salvage operations are now under way. There were negative friendly casualties and negative enemy casualties."

Arthur squinted and searched the map, looking in the area of the Tan Trang Canal for a number. A red "3". They were going to brief this incident third—last of the three major incidents. If number "2" was as relatively insignificant as "1" was, Arthur could see only one reason for not presenting the Tan Trang disaster first: McGinnis wanted to play down the loss. Wandering his eyes over the map, Arthur found the blue "2" on the Vam Co Tay River near Moc Hoa, south of the Parrot's Beak, and tuned back in to the droning briefer.

" . . . two PBRs set in night waterborne guardposts at 0450 detected a column of enemy soldiers moving along the river's edge, behind the short foliage. They were evidently unaware of the PBRs' presence . . ."

Arthur tuned out again to wonder why they called these operations "guardposts." All blue numbers represented friendly initiated action, while the red was enemy initiated. Almost all blue numbers these days were guardpost engagements. They used to be called "ambushes," but the term had been dropped in deference to a good public affairs image. So if the sailors snuck around in the dark and caught a bunch of Viet Cong moving about and killed them all, it was a successful guardpost action. If the VC caught the sailors and killed *them*, on the other hand, it was an ambush—sneaky guerilla warfare.

"Friendly casualties, none. Enemy casualties, six Victor Charlie KIA, probable. After opening fire, both PBRs got under way and moved upstream to a new guardpost position.

"At 0730 yesterday . . ." he paused, glanced from McGinnis to the Admiral and back again, then cleared his throat. "One boat of River Division 435 was ambushed in the Tan Trang Canal about three kilometers from the Vam Co Dong River." Again he paused, coughed and stepped quickly to the map and back to the podium after slapping the red "3" with his pointer. "The boat received heavy automatic weapons, small arms and B-40 rocket fire from both sides of the canal for a distance of about two kilometers.

"Enemy casualties are unknown at this time but are expected to be high since both the PBR and a Seawolf helicopter gunship expended a great deal of ordnance on active targets. There have also been reports received by Atlantic Island on the lower Vam Co River that an unknown number of civilians were killed in the incident. This information seems to be coming from a Vietnamese District Chief. It has not as yet been verified although a similar report was received by the Army MACV people up near there, at Go Dau Ha."

Admiral White fished a cigarette from its pack, lit it, threw the Zippo onto the table with a clatter, and cut in on the briefer. "We do have dead civilians up there. We know that. Just don't know how many yet. The District Chief up there is raising hell. We're sure he's a Goddamn VC sympathizer, at the very least, but still . . . That's a Free Fire Zone in there, isn't it John?"

"Yes, Admiral, it is," Captain McGinnis answered.

"Yes, huh, well those damn people don't understand things like that, I suppose. It'll cost us, I can see that already. Uh, excuse me Commander. Go ahead, please, with your briefing."

"Yessir. Thank you. Friendly Navy casualties were three KIA and two WIA, serious, including the Patrol Officer, a Lieutenant j.g. named Morelly. Jack Morelly. Lieutenant Morelly was . . . uh . . . is a veteran of numerous patrols with the Force, and already holds the Bronze Star Medal. A Seawolf of Detachment Five evacuated both WIAs to the 29th Medevac Hospital here in Binh Thuy. Also killed were one civilian, U.S., and one Army officer. Those two were both on board PBR 716 at the time. PBR 716 sank one kilometer inside the Tan Trang Canal and had to be abandoned. Salvage operations, which should not be difficult as the boat sank right at the river bank, are already underway.

"The day's fourth incident involved a Chieu Hoi Defector picked up in the Ca Mau peninsula in the area of a major PBR ambush two nights ago. Pickup of the man was made at 0420 by units of . . ."

Arthur tuned out again and passed the remainder of the briefing gazing in disbelief at the Admiral and Captain McGinnis. One boat sunk, five men dead and two badly wounded, all in a one-boat operation into a narrow canal. And these people sat through the briefing and listened as though that sort of thing happened every day. Of course, he realized, they all knew of the incident well before they entered the briefing. Obviously, they had decided not to begin ranting about it in front of all the staff officers.

As the briefing broke up, Arthur found himself jammed behind the open door as those senior to him filed out. When he finally exited the room and began to make for the obscurity of his desk, Commander Irwin called to him from outside the Captain's office.

"Yessir," Arthur answered.

"Bring those next-of-kin letters in here. You get them rewritten and typed?"

"Yessir."

"OK, bring them in."

On top of his desk the radio yeoman had placed Personnel Casualty Reports, CASREPTS as they were called, on the three dead 435 sailors. Arthur glanced at the first few lines of the top one, for it never failed to chill him the way in which the end of a human being was so routinely, electronically reported.

PERSONNEL CASREPT—01: 2045H,
26 DEC 68
1. HAGREN, WALTER H., B328 105,
BM1, USN

2. RIVDIV 435 (BOAT CAPT.)
3. KILLED IN ACTION (HOSTILE
   FIRE, DIRECT)
4. 0740h, 26 DEC 68. TAN TRANG
   CANAL, 1 KILOMETER EAST OF
   VAM CO DONG RIVER, III
   CORPS TACTICAL ZONE.
5. BODY FLOWN TO GRAVES REG-
   ISTRATION, SAIGON.

And it went on from there, listing facts surrounding the death, how he died, names of next of kin and so on. Arthur pulled the recently stowed manila folders out of his desk drawer, stuck each man's CASREPT in the back of its proper folder, and made his way through the early morning heat to the air-conditioned office. He did not have to knock, for Commander Irwin was standing beside the glass door, saw him approaching and opened the door. He closed it again quickly so as not to let the heat in or the cold out.

No one addressed Lieutenant Arthur directly, so he backed up against the closest wall and stood at what he hoped resembled some sort of erect position despite the fact that his shoulder blades were resting comfortably against the plywood bulkhead.

"I talked to NAVFORV in Saigon this morning," Admiral White was saying to McGinnis, referring to his boss, THE MAN, Admiral Zumwalt, the popular Commander of all Naval forces in Vietnam. "He wants to know what one PBR was doing running up that canal. I'd like to know that myself. We can get away with that kind of crap on the big rivers. But you know, John, it's a standing Sea Lords order that boats in these new operations run at least in pairs. The Force has always worked that way. And God knows that should go doubly for our units in places like the upper Vam Co Dong there."

"Yes, sir. I realize that."

"Well, I need to understand what your thinking was, if there was any, in allowing that. But even that hell of a mess . . . and our own losses . . . look like they'll have to take a back seat to this civilian thing. Best information we can get from MACV (the overall "Military Assistance Command" for Vietnam) in Saigon and from USARV (The Army command in the Delta) in Can Tho is thirteen civilians dead. Have you heard any differently?"

"First word we got here was by way of Atlantic Island," Captain McGinnis answered. "It was seven or eight then. What's the most recent count we've gotten from Commander Getzel, Bill?" He turned to his Deputy.

"Thirteen, Captain," Commander Irwin answered.

"Right," said Admiral White. "Well now I guess it'll be an unlucky thirteen. Have you any idea what actually happened?" The Admiral's eyes narrowed, as he looked hard at Captain McGinnis. It wasn't clear to Arthur, trying to keep himself invisible, whether the Admiral meant that he wanted the truth or if he was asking McGinnis "What's your official story going to be?"

"As nearly as we can piece together at this time," McGinnis began, "the PBR was forced to beach in a break along the tree line about one kilometer inside the Tan Trang but still within the designated Free Fire Zone. At the back of the clearing, I've got no idea how far back from the water, there was a hootch. Might have been several hootches, in fact. At any rate, if any civilians were killed it was because they were inside the hootch, or hootches. When the PBR was abandoned, there were four Americans alive. The Patrol Officer, Morelly, his Boat

Captain, a gunner and the Army officer. The Army man was not conscious at the time and he died before they could be choppered out of there. The Boat Captain was killed during the rescue itself. In the chopper, in fact. Right as they were lifting off. Lucky shot, I guess. Or unlucky.

"Probably our people were receiving fire from the hootch or hootches. At any rate, it seems they were putting M-16 fire into the hootch line, as the Seawolves arrived. The Seawolf Fire Team Leader, also a Lieutenant j.g. like the PBR officer, tried to set his ship down in the clearing and began taking fire from someplace, presumably from a hootch. He pulled up and his wing man put in a strike on the hootch. After that, the FTL made another attempted pickup. He received more fire, but still managed to get everyone out. Except for the Army officer. Had to leave him. Too much weight. His body was picked up about an hour later."

"You said he was dead, though. I mean, the Army officer. They were sure he was dead before they decided to leave him, weren't they?"

"Oh, yes, sir. He was dead. The door gunner was the one to notice it. They were too heavy to get off, so they dumped the body when they realized he was dead. Ironic, Admiral, since he was the one the PBR went in to save."

"Jesus. Dump the Army guy. Thank God there's no doubt about him already being gone."

"Yes, sir. But Admiral, there's a lot more to this mission, as I understand it, than just us maybe—maybe—wiping out some innocent civilians. And by the way, that District Chief we strongly suspect is at least a VC sympathizer. The Seals have been trying to nail him for over a month."

"I know that, John. But I don't want to hear it," replied the Admiral quickly. Most senior officers didn't necessarily want to know exactly what the Seals were up to at any given minute of the day, or night.

"Yes, sir," McGinnis went on. "Well, that wasn't really my point, sir. This was a special mission that had been checked off with Lieutenant Commander Getzel, who's Atlantic Island, in charge of Slingshot overall. I think you know him, Admiral. Annapolis, class of '59?"

The Admiral gave a vague nod. McGinnis went on. "Sir, the mission was initiated by a USAid type. Mendez was his name. He was the civilian casualty in the action. The mission was to rescue an Army chopper pilot held by the VC up the Tan Trang. This guy Mendez evidently made a deal with the VC—money changed hands." McGinnis paused and looked around the room. No one moved a muscle. He went on.

"The patrol took Mendez to a meet with a Viet Cong off Hiep Hoa. They made a deal, and the patrol was to find the prisoner—the pilot—up the Tan Trang Canal. Part of the deal was minimal firepower. One boat only, no air, no ground troops. The patrol rescued the pilot, but the whole thing then went bad somehow."

"It seems pretty obvious," Commander Irwin added. "It was a setup from the start. Admiral, we should be talking about these men like they were heroes. They WERE heroes. They went up a narrow canal, alone, to try to save one of our own."

"That's enough, Bill," Captain McGinnis cut off his subordinate.

"Gentlemen," Admiral White paused for effect. "I may have a little more background on this situation than some of you do." Another pause. For gravitas or effect? Arthur wondered, in the corner. What was coming next?

"I got a call last night from Saigon. From MACV headquarters." Every back in the room straightened up. MACV HQ was the overall military command in Vietnam. Lots of Colonels and Generals, probably a few Admirals, up to and including Westmoreland himself. "They asked me what I knew of this operation. I knew nothing, of course, at the time." He stared at McGinnis who, for the first time, dropped his head.

"Sorry, Admiral. I didn't think you needed . . ."

Admiral White cut him off and went on. "They patched me through to USAid. I don't have the man's name here. One of the spooks. Probably CIA. Talked like a pretty senior officer. He said I would be hearing more about this operation and he wanted me to know, up front, that no one from their branch had been involved."

Commander Irwin once again interjected. "Admiral, I spoke with Commander Getzel. This guy Mendez flew in to the YRBM-14 to see Getzel, briefed him, then flew up to Tra Cu, to the Special Forces camp there, to brief Lieutenant Franklin."

"I'm just telling you what Saigon is telling me, Commander," Admiral White replied.

"I understand, sir."

"So I called one of my Army buddies in Can Tho. They had lost a pilot, all right, and they were also under the impression that he was being pulled out by the Navy, by a PBR, but it seems no one there had ever heard of this guy, this Mendez. I can tell you, gentlemen . . . I feel it in my bones. We're going to get stonewalled big time if we try to trace this thing back to the spooks." Admiral

White, who had been looking mainly at McGinnis as he spoke, now turned to Commander Irwin.

"Commander, you say you spoke with Getzel?"

"Yes, Admiral. He told me about the Mendez visit, and that he had communicated with Franklin after Mendez had visited Franklin at Tra Cu. But he insists that he did not order the operation."

"Well, so who the fuck did?" Admiral White asked, raising his voice for the first time. Little shocks went through the room.

'I think, Admiral," said Irwin, now slightly cowed. "That Getzel gave Franklin authority to proceed as he saw fit."

"Franklin's the Division Commander, right?"

"Yes, Admiral."

"I met him once, didn't I, John?"

"Right. You did, sir. I believe it was here at Binh Thuy when we were briefing all the Giant Slingshot commanders, just before we kicked it off."

"Yes" said the Admiral. "I remember him. Tall man. John, you know our relations with the Vietnamese in that area are far from good. There was the Hiep Hoa burning and other incidents, and now this. They neither know nor give a damn why an American patrol boat was up that canal. All they know is that it was up there and that the end result was thirteen of their people dead. Assuming the District Chief or whomever isn't padding the figures. Anyway, our luck, it'll all be kids and old mama-sans.

"There's a hell of a lot more Army that has to operate in that area than there is Navy. Now it looks like we've busted in there, off the river which is the limit of our Op Area, and screwed up their pacification program,

medical aid programs and whatever other Goddamn programs they're running these days."

"Yessir."

"The point is, John, we can't just say '*xin loi* . . . too
bad' and pay out the 4,000 piasters per head or whatever
it is the little bastards will want from us. We've got to
take some sort of disciplinary action. Now you knew of
this operation before it was brought off?"

"Yessir."

"Well, I'm sure you're well aware of the limits of our
Op Area up on Slingshot."

"Yessir."

"Yes, and I'm sure Lieutenant Commander Getzel
over at Atlantic Island is also aware of the geography.
Where we can go and can't go and so forth. You've got
some fine division commanders, John, but I'm afraid
sometimes, and this seems to be one of those times, they
assume too much responsibility in their eagerness to do a
good job. They go a bit too far sometimes. I realize that
we give out medals for initiative and so on, above and
beyond the call. But on the other hand, when something
like this backfires, well, I don't need to tell you
something's got to give. Somewhere. If that young Division Commander up at 435, Franklin, talked to anybody here or to Getzel, he must have misunderstood
something somewhere along the line. I'm sure Getzel
didn't order him to put that boat in there."

"No, I doubt it, Admiral."

"No, of course not. Well, I think it would be wise
for us to get someone up there to 435 and relieve your
Lieutenant Franklin. What's his first name?"

Again, Captain McGinnis turned to his Deputy.
"Bill?"

"Emmitt Franklin, sir. Lieutenant Emmitt Franklin."

"Yes, Emmitt Franklin. Well, I think it best, and I'm sure you'll agree, John, that we can get someone just as capable up there to relieve him. Maybe you can send someone from the staff here, temporarily, then get an experienced combat officer from another division up there in a few days."

A loud rap on the door next to him startled Arthur. Commander Irwin pulled it open and the Captain's yeoman stepped inside.

"Yes, Rubens, what is it?"

"Excuse me, Captain, but Saigon is on the line . . ."

"OK, thank you."

"Uh, it's actually for the Admiral, sir. One of Admiral Zumwalt's aides. Line two."

McGinnis had picked up the receiver and quickly handed it across to Admiral White. "Very well, Rubens, thank you. Close that door, Bill. This damn air-conditioner's working overtime."

Admiral White sat erect on the edge of his chair and spoke quietly into the mouthpiece. Apparently too quietly.

"I said 'Yes, this is Admiral White.' Very well, put him on." He covered the mouthpiece with one hand. "It's NAVFORV. Chief Staff Officer."

McGinnis glanced quickly from White to Irwin then down at his desk.

"Yes, Captain McGraw," Admiral White began. Admirals hated to defer to lower ranking officers simply because they worked for higher ranking officers. "I can hear you loud and clear. Yes, I know. I spoke to Admiral Zumwalt earlier this morning. Yes, I'm up-to-date as far as I know. Captain McGinnis and I were just talking about it." The Admiral listened for several seconds.

"You'll have to say that again. We got a little static on the line.

"What?" White's blood pressure began to rise visibly and Arthur wished he were back in the heat and dust of the outer office. What the hell do you mean 'redesignated'? When? On the thirteenth?" White was now out of his chair, pacing the floor as far as the cord would allow him to go. "Why didn't we know about it? Just a second. John, give me a pen, will you? OK. Yeah, go ahead. NAVFORV message date-time group one-nine-three-six of thirteen December sixty-eight. Yeah, I got it." He threw the pen onto McGinnis's desk and tore the scrap of paper off the tablet. "Hold on one second, McGraw, will you?"

Admiral White covered the mouthpiece and handed the paper to Irwin. "We're in deep shit. Have your radio man dig out this message. On the double." He placed the receiver back to his head. "OK, Captain, I'm with you. Go ahead.

"Well, hell, yes I realize that this changes the complexion of the whole thing. I don't know. If Admiral Zumwalt wants me there right away I guess I could be there by noon. My chopper's down at Can Tho.

"Yes, I understand. Yes. Yes. OK, I'll have Captain McGinnis get that under way. Yes, this morning. As soon as I hang up. Tell Admiral Zumwalt that we'll get it under way this morning and I'll be in Saigon by noon. Have a car at the Tan Son Nhut Heliport to meet me. Right. Yes, see you then."

He hung up the phone slowly. A young Communications Officer barged through the door carrying a red

folder marked SECRET in stenciled letters. Captain
McGinnis looked ready to die with anxiety. He was whiter
than any sheet Arthur had seen since he had left the States.
"What is it, Admiral?"

"Give me that message folder, son. Where's this date-
time group I asked for?"

The Communications Officer tried desperately to
keep his finger in the place he had marked but White
seized the folder away from him. "Right here, Admiral.
Here it is right here. Uh, right there."

"Where? Which one?"

"That one there, sir."

"Huh, OK. Thank you."

"Yessir." The young officer wheeled and vanished,
giving Arthur a roll of his eyes as he passed by.

McGinnis was now on his feet, leaning over the desk
in an effort to see the message. "What is it, Admiral?"

"This message. Thirteen December. That's two weeks
ago. It redesignates the Tan Trang Canal area. Here, read
it."

"Redesignates it as what?" McGinnis asked, sound-
ing somehow winded.

"Read it."

McGinnis donned his reading glasses and glanced
down the message text.

"Paragraph four."

"Yes, I see." McGinnis began to read aloud. 'Due to
the highly successful nature of pacification programs on
the Tan Trang Canal near the Vam Co Dong River, there
is evidence that the rate of friendly Vietnamese resettlement in this area will rise rapidly in the coming weeks
and months. In an effort to aid this resettlement, the
area of the Tan Trang Canal from the mouth of the Vam

Co Dong River to a point five kilometers up the canal will no longer be designated a Free Fire Zone. The area will be considered to be friendly and under government control. American armed contact with civilians in this area must be avoided at all costs.'" Captain McGinnis finished reading and sat back in his chair. "Jesus Christ. Like this wasn't bad enough already."

Admiral White leaned forward and took the folder from the desk and stabbed at the end of the message. "Yes, exactly. Here, John. See. You initialed it."

"Yes, I see. I don't remember it, of course. The Tan Trang is out of our operations area up there. This didn't seem pertinent at the time."

"Yes, well, I can fully understand that," the Admiral nodded. "You've got more to do than keep watch over all your commands. What about Getzel? Oh, let's see, he didn't get a copy for some reason, according to the list of addressees here. What's-his-name did, though. Franklin. Here, he's on the list.

"I'm afraid this leaves us little alternative, John. Saigon wants a Board of Inquiry set up immediately. You'll have to get someone to relieve Lieutenant Franklin right away. Today, if possible. Get him down here temporarily. I think it's safe to say that the Force as a command is off the spot. Getzel, too, since he never got a copy of the message. Which he should have, by the way.

"At any rate, I think we can safely say that the responsibility must lie either with Lieutenant Franklin or with the Patrol Officer—the young man who was wounded. Morelly. Possibly with the Seawolf pilot as well. I don't know. Anyway, we should try to keep the thing at that level. The responsibility of the operational command actually involved and so on. I'll be back from

Saigon either tonight or tomorrow morning. I'll want to know what progress we've made."

"Yessir."

"My God, that Division 435 had done a fine job up on Slingshot until now, hadn't they?"

"Yessir. A bigger body count and more ammunition caches in the twenty days since Slingshot started than in any comparable time period in the past three years. They have been very gung ho. Very aggressive."

"Yes, well, I'll leave you all to take care of the details on this matter. Oh, the two survivors. They're just over at the 29th Evac Hospital across the street, right?"

McGinnis looked again to Bill Irwin who immediately picked up the cue. "One is, Admiral. The gunner was in good condition this morning so they moved him out to Third Field in Saigon. He'll probably go on to Japan tomorrow or the next day.

"The Patrol Officer, Jack Morelly, is still over there. Will be for a few days until he's strong enough to be moved. They had to take off part of his leg yesterday afternoon."

"Ah . . . damned shame," the Admiral sighed. "Well, John, it might be a good idea to get someone over there while, ah, while that young man's still here and see if he can give a statement."

Without waiting for a response, the Admiral rose and tugged his green fatigue cap, two gleaming white stars on its crown, down over his brow. Suddenly he noticed Arthur, in the corner, by the door.

"And what can we do for this fellow?" he said, staring at Arthur, whose position of modified attention had become significantly more regulation in the preceding tense minutes.

"I've got some condolence letters that the Commander said the Captain wanted to see, sir," replied Arthur.

"On those men killed yesterday?"

"Yes, Admiral."

"Uh huh. Have the next of kin been notified yet?"

"No sir," Arthur said, glancing over to Irwin. "We haven't received any message on it."

"We always wait until we get message confirmation that next of kin have been personally notified before we send out a condolence letter," Irwin added.

"Yes, of course. In fact, it's Saigon's policy, isn't it? Hunh. May I?"

"Yes, sir, Admiral," Arthur said as he handed the Admiral the folders, being forced to step forward and relinquish his corner as he did so.

The top folder fell to the floor in the exchange, but the Admiral didn't seem to notice. He simply opened the next one, and began reading the draft of the letter.

Commander, River Patrol Flotilla
Five
FPO San Francisco, Calif. 96627
XX December, 1968

Mr. and Mrs. Frederick J. Lemon
1050 Emerson Rd.
Haverford, Penna. 19041
Dear Mr. and Mrs. Lemon,

It is with heartfelt sympathy that I extend to you, on behalf of the officers and men of the River Patrol Force, my deepest condolences on the death of your son, Donald, who died in the service of his country in the Republic of Vietnam.

Since you naturally will have a desire to know of the circumstances surrounding your son's death, I can offer you the following information.

On the morning of 26 December 1968, Donald was serving as a machine gunner aboard a river patrol boat on a routine operation along the Tan Trang Canal, about thirty miles northwest of Saigon. In the course of the operation, the patrol was taken under heavy rocket and automatic weapons fire by a numerically superior enemy force dug in along both sides of the canal. In the firefight that ensued, Donald defended his boat to the limit, responding courageously to the situation until finally being struck by enemy gunfire. He died instantly, without suffering.

Although I did not know Donald personally, I was well aware of the excellent record he had established within his unit. His courage and determination will be an inspiration to us all.

If I can be of further assistance to you in any way, please do not hesitate to contact me.

Sincerely,
John A. McGinnis
Captain, U.S. Navy

"Yes, I see," the Admiral nodded, motioning Arthur to his side. "This a pretty standard letter, Ensign?"

"Yes, sir," Arthur answered. "Every situation is different, Admiral, of course. But we, uh, we try to make the letter something that the family can, well, sir, that they can feel some pride in."

"In that second paragraph," Captain McGinnis interjected, "we decided to say 'on a routine operation along the Tan Trang Canal'. It had been 'on a critical mission'."

"Yes, I see. That's good. But here, young man," the Admiral spoke to Arthur out of the side of his mouth. "'Taken under heavy rocket and automatic weapons fire by a numerically superior enemy force dug in along both sides of the canal.' Sounds like a Goddamn suicide mission or something. You see what I mean, son?"

"Yes sir, Admiral," Arthur answered dutifully.

"You see what I mean, John?"

"Yes, Admiral."

"Let's change that to something like 'they were taken under fire by an enemy force of unknown strength' or something to that effect. You know what I mean, son. You could probably put it much better than I could. You're the writer."

"Certainly, Admiral," Arthur answered.

"All those letters have that part in them, Arthur?" McGinnis asked.

"Yes, sir, I believe so."

"You believe so?"

"Yessir, they do."

"OK, well, have them all written over again and let me see them as soon as they're done."

"Yessir."

"That's all."

Arthur took back the files, picked up the Hagren file that was still on the floor, took one giant pace backward, did an about-face, and headed for the door.

"Oh, John," the Admiral raised a forefinger in hesitation. "Just one more thing. Wait a moment, son." Arthur stopped in his tracks and about-faced once again. "Saigon will be asking about medals for those young men. You ought to get your writer here to work something up."

"Of course, Admiral. Mr. Arthur, how long will it take for you to work up citations for the boat crew and the Patrol Officer?"

"Uh, John, perhaps you ought to hold off on a recommendation for the Patrol Officer. At least for a few days. Let's maybe see which way the wind's going to blow on this thing."

"Yes, Admiral, of course. That would be wise. How long will it take you to write citations for the crew, Arthur?"

"It depends on how high you want to go, sir."

"Oh, hell, I don't know. What do we usually do with something like this?"

"We generally recommend the Bronze Star for a man killed in action, sir."

"All right, let's make the three posthumous awards Bronze Stars. Hell, that last kid was damn-near killed. Write up all four of them for Bronze Stars. How's that?"

"Yes, sir."

"That sound OK?"

"Yes, sir."

"OK. That's all then."

Arthur turned again, without speaking further, and started toward the door, only to be caught by Commander Irwin. "Right after lunch you'd better take my jeep and get over to the 29th Evac Hospital. Try and get a statement of some kind before they move Jack Morelly out to Japan."

"Yes, sir." Ensign Arthur did not have to take his eyes off the gray concrete floor to see the lack of conviction on the face of Commander Irwin, one of the few senior officers he had come to admire during his brief Naval career. What kind of a statement could they expect from a young officer who had just lost his boat, his crew and his leg? Were they going to try to pin something other than a medal on Lieutenant Morelly?

Arthur stood outside the Commodore's office door for a moment, allowing the last cool wisps of conditioned air to wash over him before the withering Asian heat hit him. He scribbled corrections on the top letter as he walked slowly to a bank of desks where a row of T-shirted sailors typed away on one piece or another of official correspondence. Arthur threw the folders onto his yeoman's desk.

"Aw, Christ, Mr. Arthur, you gonna make me do them over again?"

"Yes, Branson. Again. All of them. The changes are on the Lemon letter."

The young man shook his head in frustration. "Mr. Arthur, why don't you tell those people to make up their minds the first fucking time?"

"Just get the letters done, Branson, huh? No lip. I don't need it right now."

"Yeah, OK, Mr. Arthur. But it's not like I got nothing else to do. Look at all this crap I gotta get out. I don't know. You gotta wonder sometimes. You really gotta wonder how one war can get so fucked up."

"Zip it, Branson!" Arthur snapped. "This is a big deal. It's gonna be a big deal, anyway. These guys were heroes. A bad mission, but they were heroes. Just do the letters, OK?"

"Yes, sir. I'm sorry, sir." Branson replied. He spoke quietly, to no one in particular, still shaking his head. "They're all heroes when they're fucking dead."

All profits from this book are being donated to organizations that support veterans of the Navy's River Patrol Force in Vietnam, and to the Police and Fire Departments of Bedford, New York.